NOAH

Susan Fisher-Davis

D1501660

Men of Clifton, Montana
Book 22

Erotic Romance

Noah Men of Clifton, Montana Book 22
Copyright © 2022 Susan Fisher-Davis
First Print book Publication: February 2022
ISBN: 9798416459673
Cover Artist: Untold Designs Romance and Fantasy Covers
Cover Model: Jeremy Allison
Cover Photographer: Golden Czermak
Edited By: Red Sky Editing
All cover art copyright © 2022 by Susan Davis

PUBLISHER: Blue Whiskey Publishing
Webpage: https://susanfisherdavisauthor.weebly.com

Acknowledgments

To my betas, Renee, Alison, and Holly—you ladies are the
best, and I appreciate you all.

To my husband, Rob—I love you!

To Jeremy Allison for being Noah. I knew
when I saw this photo, you were perfect for it.

You can find Jeremy on Instagram at:

@jeremyallisonfitness

To Golden Czermak for the photo. You are
truly an amazing person.

You can find Golden's photos at

www.furiousfotog.com and

facebook.com/furiousfotog

To the ladies in my Facebook group: Susan's
Hot Cowboys—you make it fun.

As always to you, my readers.
I wouldn't be able to do this without you. I
love every one of you
and I appreciate your support.
From the bottom of my heart, thank you.

Chapter One

Once he finished rubbing the saddle down, Noah Conway looked at it and grinned. It looked great. He'd give the customer a call to tell him it was ready. This one took a lot of work because the client wanted it for his daughter, and Noah had to add purple stitching. He also stitched her name on the cantle. Arching his back, he knew he would be spending a little time in the hot tub. Standing all day while working on saddles always put a kink in his back. He stepped to the sink and washed his hands.

The weather had cooled, and he knew that soon the snow would blanket the little towns of Clifton, Spring City, and Hartland. It was late September.

He strode out of his workroom and down the aisle of the barn. Since he was sixteen, he'd been making saddles by hand, and his craftsmanship only perfected over the years. People from across the states ordered saddles and tack from him. They were also sold in retail stores, but many people wanted one directly from him. A Conway saddle was second to none. He stayed busy. One of his barns held only equipment to make the tack.

He was also a guide for hunting elk and mule deer in Kalispell during the fall and winter months. He owned twelve hundred acres and had several cabins built for hunters, along with a lodge where meals were served. Soon, it would be time to take hunters up into the mountains.

His one rule was that they hunt for meat, not trophies. He'd never believed in killing an animal just for the sport of it and wasting meat.

Two other guides worked for him, so he could continue to work on saddles, but he took two weeks off in late November to take hunting parties and hunt himself. He wished he could go more often, but he had too many orders. Since he made them by hand, he took a while to complete an order. It didn't bother him though, he loved working with his hands and loved the finished product as much as the customers did.

The hunters would be met at the cabins the week of the hunt. Eight hunters were the limit, so he could keep an eye on them. They would ride horses up into the mountains. Noah's land butted up to a National Park, but no hunting was allowed in the Park, so only his land was hunted. He was already booked through the entire season.

Archery season ran from September seventh through October twentieth, and rifle season was October twentieth through November. Mule deer and elk seasons were both in simultaneously. Hunters could hunt either or both.

The cold air made him pick up his pace when he stepped into the sunshine. He walked across the yard, jogged up the steps, wiped his feet, opened the door, and entered the kitchen, sighing at the warmth. His Border collies, Sparky, and Spike, sat staring up at him.

Grinning, he took his hat off and hung it up, then he pulled a chair out from the kitchen table, took a seat, and toed off his boots. Picking them up, he pushed to his feet and carried the boots into the mudroom. He set them inside the door, then reentered the kitchen and stared at the dogs.

"I suppose because you think you're being good, you deserve biscuits," he said, grinning. The dogs knew not to do anything until he said they could, but their ears perked up at the mention of a biscuit.

They patiently sat on the rug, waiting for their master to pet them. Noah reached down and rubbed both their ears, then they stood and spun in circles. Turning, he reached into the box sitting by the door and handed them each a biscuit. Although the box sat open, they never took from it.

After giving them the treats, he headed for the bathroom to take a hot shower. He always needed one after working on the saddles, and sometimes after a shower, he'd hit the hot tub. The hot water relaxed him so much that when he'd climb out of it, he would have to get into bed, and he would fall asleep.

He strode down the hallway to his bedroom and entered the bathroom, where he stripped off his jeans, boxer briefs, T-shirt, and socks, then tossed everything into the hamper. Opening the door to the shower stall, he turned the water on, and steam filled the room. The front was glass with a door centered between a panel on each side, and the three walls were ceramic tile. There was a shower head on each sidewall.

Stepping inside, he moaned as the hot water hit between his shoulder blades. Picking up the shampoo, he squirted some in his hand then scrubbed his hair. After rinsing it, he reached for the soap and scrubbed his tired body clean. He shut the water off, opened the shower door, took a navy blue towel from the rack, ran it over his hair, then down his body. He wrapped it around his waist and made his way to the mirror over the sink. Swiping his hand across it to see, he picked up the shaving cream, applied it to his face, then picked up his razor and shaved.

Scarlett had been on his mind all day today. Damn it. He couldn't shake her from his head. Should he make a trip to Dewey's tonight? He'd like to see her again. It had been a week since he'd been in the bar. Not that he spent a lot of time there, but there were times he just wanted to have a cold beer and listen to some country music. Oh, and maybe pick up a woman for sex. He wouldn't mind picking up Scarlett for sex.

"Ouch," he muttered as he nicked his chin with the blade.

After he finished, he rinsed his face to rid it of the remaining shaving cream then splashed on aftershave.

After whipping off the towel and hanging it on a rack, he entered the bedroom, pulled on a clean T-shirt, a pair of sweatpants, and headed for the kitchen to get some food into him. It was Friday, and if he weren't too tired after he ate, he'd make a trip to town and have a beer. He just hoped Scarlett was there.

****

Scarlett Robinson could not get over the crowd in the bar. Didn't these people have anything else to do? Not that she should complain. They were spending money, and that was good. She just never realized how packed the place got.

The band was loud, and the dance floor was wall-to-wall people. Either in line dances or just dancing. Cowboy hats were everywhere you looked, from the dance floor to the poolroom and lined along the bar. She glanced over when the door opened and groaned when more people entered.

"I heard that."

She turned to see her uncle standing behind her and smiled.

"Heard what?" she asked as innocently as she could while batting her eyelashes.

"That groan when you saw more people come in. You're the one who wanted to buy the place." Dewey grinned.

"Just what would all of these people do if I hadn't and the bar closed?"

Dewey laughed. "I'm sure someone would buy it. I just don't want you to regret it."

Scarlett looped her arm through his and nodded. "I won't."

"Good. I know I'm leaving it in good hands then." He looked over her shoulder at the door. "Looks like a busy night."

Scarlett glanced at the door and did a double-take when she saw her new friends enter. They laughed and talked as they passed by the bar and waved at her and Dewey. Then she watched as they pulled tables together and took their seats.

"I'll get their orders. I love that bunch," she said with a smile.

"They're a good group of women. I'm glad you got to know them." Dewey walked off to take orders along the bar.

Scarlett headed for the women, then stopped beside the table and smiled as she heard them laughing.

"Hey, Scarlett," Olivia Stone said to her. "This is Hailey Beckett. She wasn't with us the last time. Hailey, this is Scarlett Robinson. She's Dewey's niece, and she now owns the bar."

"Hi, Hailey. It's nice to meet you. What can I get everyone?"

As each woman told her what they wanted, Scarlett wrote it down. She mentally shook her head and laughed at the things they were saying. What a wonderful group of women, and she was happy to call them her friends. Each one of them handed her their purse because she kept them in a safe in the back office for them.

"Okay, I'll get these drinks for you. Go hit the dance floor," she said and headed for the bar to give the bartenders the orders, then carried the purses to the office. She squatted down in front of the safe and entered the combination. She knew it would be a few minutes before their drinks would be ready since the bartenders were busy keeping up with people lining the bar and the orders the servers gave them.

Scarlett reentered the barroom and watched her friends in a line dance laughing and having a great time. She would love to join them, but it was way too busy to take a break and dance.

An hour later, she set a beer down in front of a cowboy then turned to see Noah Conway sitting at the bar talking to Hailey Beckett. A stab of jealousy hit her when they laughed together. She took a deep breath. She had no claim on Noah. She moved to wipe up the bar in front of him.

10

"What can I get you, Noah?" she asked him, and her heart hit her stomach when he turned those honey-colored eyes at her.

"A beer is fine, Scarlett. Whatever's on tap," he said as his eyes met hers.

"I'm heading back to the table." Hailey hopped down from the stool, kissed Noah's cheek, and turned to leave but looked back when Noah spoke.

"All right. Behave yourself tonight," Noah said with a grin.

"Where's the fun in that, big brother?" Hailey winked at Scarlett, then pushed through the crowd.

Big brother? Thank God!

Scarlett watched her, then turned to Noah to see him staring at her. Heat filled her cheeks as she stared back. The man was sexy as hell.

"I'll, uh, get your beer, Noah. I'll be right back." She moved away but hesitated when he spoke in a low tone.

"Can't wait, darlin'."

She moved to the tap, removed a frozen glass then put it under the spout to pour the beer. So Hailey was his sister. Scarlett smiled then shook her head. She should have seen the resemblance. Especially their eyes.

"You have no right to be jealous," she muttered.

"What?"

She turned to see Marie, one of the servers, frowning at her.

Scarlett laughed and shook her head. "Nothing. Just talking to myself."

"God, I've been there. Oh, I see Noah Conway

11

is here. Damn, that man is so hot. I'd love to take him home."

Scarlett swore when she put too much beer in the glass, and it spilled over the top. She jumped back to keep it from getting on her, then set it down and grabbed a bar rag.

"You okay?" Marie asked her.

"Just hunky-dory," she snapped. *Again, no right to be jealous, Scarlett.* She chastised herself. Who Noah Conway took home was none of her business, but if Marie took him home, Scarlett would find a reason to fire her. Mentally shaking her head, she knew she couldn't do that. What woman wouldn't want the man? Between those eyes and his pitch-black hair, he was just gorgeous. She could admit she wanted him.

She poured some of the foam from the beer, then after wiping the glass, she headed for Noah to see him talking with another man.

"Here you go, Noah," she said as she set his beer on the bar. Then she looked at the other man and almost groaned. What the hell was it with this town? He was hot too. "What can I get you?"

"Beer is fine. Whatever is on tap," he said with a grin.

"Sure." She smiled.

"This is Dominic Blackstone, Dom, Scarlett Robinson," Noah introduced them.

Scarlett stuck her hand over the bar to him, and he took it.

"Nice to meet you, Scarlett," Dominic said.

She couldn't help but stare at him. With his black hair and eyes as dark as pitch, he had that brooding cowboy thing down to an art. She cleared her throat.

"Nice to meet you too, Dominic. I'll be right back with your beer." She grinned then turned to head for the cooler to remove a frosted mug.

****

"Back the fuck off, Blackstone," Noah growled out, then clenched his jaw when Dom laughed.

"Why the hell would I want to do that? That is one beautiful woman."

"Because I saw her first," Noah snapped.

"What are you? Ten? Hell, Noah, you could have any woman in here—"

"I want that one."

Dom shook his head. "Of course, you do."

Noah turned on the stool to look at his friend and placed his arm on the bar.

"I suppose you want her?"

Dom shrugged. "I'll back off since you...saw her first."

"Fuck you," Noah snapped but grinned when Dom chuckled.

The two men sat at the bar and talked until closing time. Noah waved a bartender over and paid his tab. As he drove home, he thought back to the first night he met Scarlett two months ago...

Dewey's sure packed them in on Friday and Saturday nights. Sitting on a stool, he turned the beer bottle around, watching it make wet circles on the bar from the condensation. He spun around on the stool and looked at the crowd.

Placing his elbows on the bar behind him, he watched the people on the dance floor. He grinned as he watched a line of them dancing to the band playing an old Kentucky Headhunters' song, *Walk Softly On This Heart Of Mine.*

Then he straightened up when he spotted the redhead making her way through the tables and setting drinks down. He peered around the crowd and tried to watch her, but some cowboys were in his way. He got to his feet and glanced around. He'd lost her. Who the hell was she? She had to be one of the servers since she'd been carrying that big round tray.

Retaking his seat, he turned around and smiled when he saw her behind the bar. Damn, she was gorgeous and built like a brick shithouse. His damn groin tightened just looking at her. Her wavy, red hair hung past her shoulders, and she wore the outfit all the female servers wore. Short, denim bibbed overalls with a gray muscle shirt underneath and cowboy boots on her feet. Even though she was petite, she had long legs, and hell, he'd love to have them wrapped around his waist. Been a long time since a woman interested him like this. He wanted her. *Now.*

She turned and looked in his direction, and their eyes met and held. He watched her take a deep breath, walk to him, and stop on the other side of the bar in front of him.

"Can I get you another beer, cowboy?"

Her sexy voice had him thinking all kinds of nasty thoughts, and he wanted her to whisper them in his ear while he took her over the edge. He grinned.

"Sure, I'll have another one. What's your name, darlin'?"

"Scarlett Robinson, and you are?"

"Noah Conway. How long have you worked

14

here?"

"Almost three months. Dewey is my uncle, and he sold the bar to me."

"Well, that means I'll see more of you. Lucky for me. Looks like I should have been coming in more often," Noah said as he lifted the bottle to his lips and drained what was left of the beer.

She leaned over the bar and smiled. He stared into those beautiful light gray eyes.

"Maybe lucky for me too, Noah." She winked, and he wanted to have sex with her on the bar. She turned from him to get him another beer, and he ran his eyes down over the back of her. *Son of a bitch.* She got his beer then headed back to him. Scarlett Robinson was a man's wet dream.

"You're not from Clifton, though, are you?"

"No. I'm from Missoula. Uncle Dewey and I have always been close. In the summer months, I would spend time with him and Aunt Ella, and he'd bring me here when he came in to do inventory or clean up the place. I loved the atmosphere of it, even at a young age. I think that was why I got into bartending. When he told me he was going to retire and sell the bar, I offered to buy it." She shrugged. "My dream has been to own a bar."

"Well, I'm glad you decided to buy this one," Noah said with a grin.

"Here you go," she said as she placed the bottle in front of Noah on the bar.

"Thanks," he said. "Did your parents name you Scarlett because of that hair?"

She laughed. "No. My mom just liked the name."

15

"Is it natural?" Noah smirked.

Scarlett leaned toward him. "Yes," she said in a low tone of voice.

"Care to prove that?"

"You, Noah Conway, are a force to be reckoned with," she said with a smile.

"You have no idea, darlin'." He picked up the bottle, took a long pull, and spun around on the stool to watch the crowd when she moved away to wait on another cowboy.

As the night wore on, he didn't get to talk to Scarlett much because she was so busy. Finally, she walked to him, set a beer on the bar in front of him, and smiled.

A young cowboy took the stool next to him and nodded.

"Hey, how about me, sugar," the cowboy beside him said.

"What would you like?" she asked the young cowboy.

"How about you?" He laughed and elbowed Noah.

Noah frowned and looked at Scarlett. She gave a tightlipped smile to the cowboy.

"I'm not on the menu. Do you want something to drink?"

"Oh, come on, sugar. I think you and I could have some fun."

"No, thank you. If you don't want to order, I'll move on."

"Hey, as long as I have a face, you have a place to sit, sugar," the cowboy said with a laugh.

"Don't be so fucking crude," Noah snapped.

Scarlett started to move away when the cowboy reached out and wrapped his fingers around her wrist.

Noah shot to his feet and glared down at the kid. He knew he was intimidating as hell. He stood six foot five in his bare feet and weighed two hundred and twenty pounds without an ounce of fat.

"She said no. Back the fuck off," he said through clenched teeth.

"It's all right, Noah. I can handle this one," she said.

He looked at her, back to the cowboy, and resumed his seat. He watched as she jerked her wrist from the young cowboy.

"Don't ever touch me again, or I will have you removed from the bar and ban you from it."

The cocky cowboy laughed. "How the hell can you ban me?"

"Because I own it, dickhead."

"Your name's Dewey?" The cowboy laughed.

"Dewey happens to be my uncle," Scarlett said.

"So, how can you own it then?"

"You're one stupid son of a bitch," Noah muttered.

"You need to back the fuck off, cowboy."

Noah got to his feet again. "I'm one man you don't want to push...*boy.*"

"I'm not a boy."

"Then quit acting like some horny little teenager. You need to learn some manners around women."

"I'll kick your ass," the cowboy said as he stared up at him.

"Don't run your mouth if you can't back up what it's saying," Noah growled out.

The kid straightened up, narrowed his eyes at him, and pushed Noah hard, making him go back against the bar.

Swearing under his breath, he righted himself just in time for the cowboy to punch him on the chin. He wrapped his hand around the back of the kid's head and slammed his face onto the bar, knocking him out and making him fall to the floor. Blood poured from his nose.

"That's enough," a deep voice said from behind him. Noah turned to see Deputy Nevada Shelton standing there.

"I didn't start it, Nevada," he told him.

Nevada frowned at him, squatted down, and tapped the cowboy on his cheek.

"Come on, wake up," Nevada said.

The kid's eyes opened, and he looked up at Nevada.

"He hit me," he said, pointing to Noah. He put his hand to his bloody nose. "He broke my nose."

"Your nose isn't broken," Noah said.

The young cowboy touched his nose again.

"How the hell would you know that?"

Noah pointed to the slight bump on his nose. "Does this look like I wouldn't know? Quit being a pussy."

Noah watched as Nevada glanced up at him, back to the cowboy on the floor, and blew out a breath.

"I suppose you want to press charges," Nevada said.

"Hell yeah, I do." The kid struggled to get to his feet. He almost passed out again until a group of his buddies came to his aid.

"What's your name?" Nevada asked him.

"Jayden Powers," he told him while holding his hand over his nose.

Nevada looked at Noah. "Come on, Noah, I have to take you in."

"Are you fucking kidding me? This little shit punched me first. Ask Scarlett. Hell, ask anyone in here." He pointed to the people sitting at the bar. They all nodded then he turned to look at Scarlett.

"He's right, Nevada. This kid started it. He grabbed me, and Noah took up for me, and this kid got pissed. He pushed Noah and punched him. Noah was just defending himself."

"Is that right?" Nevada asked the young man.

"I don't remember."

Noah laughed. "Oh, now your memory's gone, but you wanted to press charges. For what?"

"I remember you hitting me."

"I didn't hit you. Your face hit the bar." Noah cleared his throat when Nevada looked at him with a glare. "Sorry," he muttered.

Nevada turned to the kid. "I sure as hell hope you aren't driving because I can smell the alcohol on you."

"I'm not driving."

Noah watched as Nevada looked over the group of friends. "So, who is? You all look drunk to me. If I see any of you behind the wheel, your ass will be going in. We clear?"

"Yes, sir," the group muttered.

"I suggest you stop drinking, sober up, then get the hell out of here."

The group nodded, and all of them but Powers made their way back to a table. The young cowboy glared at Noah, then glanced at Nevada,

19

talking to Scarlett.

"This ain't over. Be careful when you leave."

Noah stepped forward. "You threatening me?"

"Just stating a fact. You might have taken me down, but you can't take on five of us."

"Don't bet on it. Maybe you're the one who should watch his back." Noah glared at him.

"We'll see." The young man said with a smirk.

Noah watched the punk walk away and take a seat at a table with his friends. All of them looked at him, so he saluted them, then took his place at the bar. Nevada moved to stand alongside him.

"Be careful. I have a feeling they're not going to let this go."

"I agree. What are you doing on the night shift?"

"Paul's on vacation. I told Sam I'd take it."

"How's Courtney?" Noah smiled when Nevada grinned.

"Wonderful. I'm going to look around a little, then head out. Watch your back."

"I will. Thanks, Nevada," Noah said. Nevada gave him a nod, then moved through the crowd.

"Next beer is on me." Scarlett smiled at him.

"No need. Any man should stand up for a woman. I know you can handle yourself, but he shouldn't have touched you at all. Little punk."

Scarlett placed her folded arms on the bar, leaned forward, and smiled at him. It took all his willpower not to look down at her cleavage.

"Thanks for coming to my rescue. You're my hero."

He laughed. "Sure, I am."

"Noah, I can handle myself, or I wouldn't have

bought this bar."

"I know. But my mama would kick my ass if I hadn't said something."

Scarlett smiled. "You're a good man, Noah Conway."

"I try to be."

When she lightly touched the slight bump on his nose, he swore he felt it to his toes.

"Just how did you get this?"

He smirked. "In a bar fight when I was twenty-two. I was just like him, all cocky and thought I could take on anyone." He shook his head. "I got the hell beat out of me."

Scarlett laughed and leaned over the bar again. He clenched his fists because, again, he had to keep his eyes off her breasts, straining that muscle shirt, and those shorts barely covered her ass, and what a fine ass it was. The female servers might wear the same attire, but none had him wanting a woman as fast as she did, and he just met her. Shit. He pushed the beer away, got to his feet, and removed his wallet from the back pocket of his jeans. He tossed a twenty on the bar and waved away the change.

"Thank you, Noah," Scarlett said as she picked up the money.

"I hope I see you again, Scarlett Robinson." He touched the brim of his hat, turned, and made his way through the crowd heading for the doors.

He had been back quite a lot since that night. Scarlett constantly invaded his thoughts, and he swore he'd been hard since he met her. Damn, he wanted her.

"Just ask her out," he muttered. "Chicken shit."

Shaking his head, he knew he should, but he also knew he didn't need another damn heartache. Been there. Done that. But damn, she was so sexy, and he wanted her in his bed. The sooner, the better. She could turn him on with a look.

The following Saturday, Noah entered the bar and shook his head. It was wall-to-wall people. The bar was lined up, the tables full, and the dance floor crowded. Shit. Where was he supposed to sit? As soon as that thought entered his head, a cowboy vacated a stool, and Noah took it. He looked behind the bar but didn't see Scarlett, only Laura Carson. Damn. Was she off tonight? Just his fucking luck. He smiled when Laura saw him and headed for him.

"Hi, Noah, what can I get you?"

"Beer, please." He told her what beer he wanted, watched as she walked over to the cooler, slid the door open, removed a bottle, and headed back to him. She twisted the cap off then set the bottle in front of him.

"Thanks, Laura."

"Sure, just wave me down if you want something else."

"Uh, Laura? Where's Scarlett?"

Laura glanced around. "I think she's in her office."

"Oh, okay."

Laura smiled, folded her arms on the bar, and stared at him.

"You can go back there if you want. No one else is in there right now."

"Why would I do that?"

Laura straightened up. "You, Noah Conway,

are one hardheaded man. If you're attracted to her, go for it. I know she's attracted to you. You two just need to stop dancing around each other. The office is in the hallway down from the restrooms."

Noah's jaw went slack, but he clenched his teeth together before his mouth dropped open. Scarlett was attracted to him? Well, hell. He pushed to his feet, smiled at Laura, walked along the bar, and at the end, he turned and headed down a hallway. He stopped in front of the door with *Office* above it, took a deep breath, and knocked.

"Come in," Scarlett called out.

He reached for the knob, turned it, and entered the room. He saw her sitting at a desk with her head down, looking over some papers.

"What is it?" she asked without looking up.

Noah leaned back against the door, folded his arms, and grinned.

"I came to see you," he said.

Her head snapped up, her eyes widened, and a smile lit up her beautiful face. She tossed the pen she'd been holding onto the top of the desk, leaned back in the chair, and folded her arms.

"Is that right?"

"Yes, are you okay with that?"

She shoved the chair back, got to her feet, walked around the desk, strode to him, and stopped within feet of him, and smiled up at him.

"I'm more than okay with it, Noah."

He couldn't take his eyes off her as she stood there staring up at him. He was a hell of a lot taller than she was, but damn, she was so fucking sexy. He grinned.

"I'm glad to hear that," he said right before he wrapped his hands around her biceps, pulled her close, and lowered his head. He hovered his lips above hers. "Can I kiss you?" he whispered.

"Yes—"

He cut her words off by pressing his lips to her soft ones. She opened to him, and he slid his tongue into her mouth and groaned when she moved hers against his. Her arms slipped around his waist, and she pressed herself against him. His damn dick rose in record time. She pulled back from him and stared into his face.

"What took you so long?" she asked him.

He blew out a laugh. "Hell if I know."

When she laughed, he pressed his lips to hers again. He moved his hands down her back to her ass, cupped it in his hands, and lifted her. She wrapped her legs around his waist and moved against him.

"Damn, Scarlett, you're going to make me embarrass myself. I want you so much. I have since I first saw you."

"Stay after we close. I live upstairs," she whispered in his ear, nipped the lobe with her teeth, then moved her lips back close to his.

"All right," he said before taking her lips again.

****

Scarlett had never been kissed like this. It was a toe-curling kiss, and she wanted so much more with this man. She wasn't a slut by any means, but Noah Conway had her burning up from the minute she had first laid eyes on him. She slowly pulled her lips from his and looked into those beautiful eyes.

"Once we close, I'll show you my apartment,"

she said with a grin.

Noah huffed out a laugh. "I hope that includes the bedroom, darlin'. I've never wanted a woman so much." He placed his forehead against hers.

"I feel the same about you," she whispered.

"Good." He let her down then quickly kissed her lips.

"I want you to know something, Noah."

"What's that?"

"I'm not shy in bed," she said, grinning.

"Good, because I'm not either." He gave her a quick kiss. "I'll be at the bar."

"All right."

He touched the brim of his hat, turned, opened the door then walked out. Scarlett leaned her forehead against the door, took deep breaths, and then jumped back when someone knocked on it. She opened it to see Laura standing there with a grin on her face.

"What?" Scarlett said as heat poured into her cheeks.

"Seriously? It's about time he made a move. He's been watching you any time he was here."

"You're imagining things."

"Nope. Let me tell you this, I have been working here for a few years now, and I can count on one hand how many times Noah has been in here, and he has surpassed that number since seeing you."

"He has heartbreaker written all over him." Scarlett groaned.

"He's a damn good man, but he has been hurt in the past, so take your time with him."

"Hurt? How?"

"He's been engaged three times."

"What?" Scarlett was shocked.

"Yeah, I'm not sure what happened that he didn't marry any of them, but maybe it was because he was waiting for you," Laura said with a smile.

"I'm not ready to settle down either, so maybe we can just have some fun together."

"Good for you. As I said to Noah, you two have been dancing around each other for months. Let's get back out there. We're busy." Laura opened the door, and they both strode out.

Scarlett thought it best not to look at Noah for the rest of the night. He was just too much of a temptation. Was she crazy for asking him to stay with her? She didn't know him well. She glanced over at him to see him staring at her, and a corner of those sexy lips rose in a smirk. No, she didn't know him well, but she sure wanted to.

Chapter Two

Noah sat at the bar and glanced at his watch. *Again.* Damn, why the hell wasn't it closing time yet? He needed to get that woman upstairs and hopefully into her bed. He wouldn't pressure her. He wasn't that kind of man. If it happened, great. If not, he'd go home and probably have a hard-on all damn night.

Since cooler weather had set in, she wore jeans, a T-shirt, and cowboy boots, instead of the outfit she wore in the hotter months. It didn't matter. Those jeans looked as if they'd been painted on, but he would do his best to talk her out of them.

He watched her move around behind the bar making drinks or getting someone a beer. Not once did she look his way. Laura waited on him. He didn't have a problem with Laura, but he would rather have Scarlett wait on him so he could talk to her a little.

Huffing out a breath, he spun around on the stool and watched the people on the dance floor.

"Hi," a soft voice said from beside him.

Noah looked over to see a stunning blonde woman smiling at him. He nodded.

"Ma'am."

"Do you mind if I sit here?"

"No, ma'am." He turned his gaze back to the dance floor.

"My name is Charlene," she said and stuck her hand out to him.

"Noah," he said as he shook her hand.

She was a real beauty, but he had no interest in her. He was only interested in the redhead behind the bar.

"Buy me a drink?"

He hesitated. He didn't want her getting ideas.

"Sure, but I have to tell you, darlin', that I'm not interested in anything more."

"Is that right?" She ran her finger along his arm. "Maybe I could change your mind."

Noah chuckled. "No doubt you could, but not tonight."

"Another beer, Noah?"

He turned around on the stool and saw Scarlett standing there.

"No, thanks, Scarlett. I think I'd like to keep my wits about me for...later," he said with a wink, making her grin.

Scarlett leaned over the bar. "You'll need them."

"Hell," he muttered, making her laugh.

"Oh, I see. Okay, well, I didn't mean to step on anyone's toes. You two have a nice night." Charlene looked at Scarlett. "Lucky woman." Then she disappeared through the crowd and onto the next cowboy.

Noah grinned. "I think you ran her off."

Scarlett straightened up. "If you'd rather—"

"Nope. I had already told her I wasn't interested, but she didn't seem to take the hint. I think you sealed the deal."

"I just wanted to remind you that you made plans with me."

"No need to remind me, sweetheart. I'm looking forward to it."

"Me too." She winked then moved away to wait

on people at the bar.

Hell, could this damn bar just close? He was sure he'd been hard since he kissed her. He shifted in his seat, just thinking about getting her upstairs.

Finally, he watched Laura ring the bell behind the bar and shout it was last call. Thank God! One more hour. He glanced at his watch and then saw people ordering more drinks. They shouldn't be drinking and driving, but he was sure there were cops out there just waiting. Why did they all feel they needed one more for the road?

Noah knew a few deputies would be out there. Sam Garrett didn't tolerate drinking and driving in his county, and Noah knew Grayson Beckett didn't in his either. Both men were tough sheriffs in their counties.

As he watched people finally filing out, along with the employees, he turned to see Scarlett walking to the double entrance doors and locking them. He spun around on the stool and kept his eyes on her. She turned around, leaned back against the doors with her arms behind her, and smiled at him.

"You're killing me," he said as he got to his feet and strode to her. He stopped within inches of her and stared down into her face.

"I sure don't want to do that, Noah Conway." She stood on her toes and tried to kiss him, but she was too short.

He chuckled. "You can't even reach my chin."

"I can kiss you everywhere else, though," she whispered, and he swore his dick went hard in an instant.

29

"Damn, Scarlett." He wrapped his hands around her biceps, pulled her against him, lowered his head, and took her lips in a hard kiss. Her arms wound around his neck. He lifted her, and her legs wrapped around his waist. She slowly pulled her lips from his.

"I want you, Noah. Let's go upstairs."

He set her on her feet. "Should we clean up? I noticed you sent everyone home."

"I told them I'd take care of it tomorrow."

"Well, then, lead the way, darlin'."

She smiled up at him, took his hand in hers, and led him through the bar. She turned lights out as she did, then led him down the hallway to a door. After she unlocked it, she opened it, took his hand again, and led him up the stairs.

"Do you need to lock that?"

"No, it locks automatically."

"Okay," he said and had a hell of a time keeping his eyes off her ass as she moved up the steps.

At the top of the stairs, she unlocked another door, shoved it open, turned around, and backed into the room while tugging on his hand. Hell, she didn't need to pull him in; he was going willingly.

Once inside, she closed the door. He saw two doorways to the left of the kitchen. Noah glanced around the apartment. It was small but nice. A large sofa sat facing a flatscreen TV with an overstuffed chair beside it. A coffee table sat centered in front of the couch, and the kitchen sat behind it and was small.

"I know it's little, but I like being able to live above the bar," she said.

He turned to look at her. "It's a nice little place. I never knew it was up here."

"Uncle Dewey used it for storage, so once I decided to buy the bar, I cleaned it up. It has one bedroom and one bath, but what more does one person need?"

"True. I've never asked, but just how is Dewey your uncle?"

"He's my mother's brother." Scarlett stared up at him.

Noah stepped closer to her, cupped her face in his hands, and lowered his lips to hers then slowly raised them. "Want to show me the bedroom?"

"Yes," she said, took his hand again, and led him to one door. "That is the bathroom." She pointed to the door on the opposite wall.

"Not interested in that one right now."

Scarlett smiled at him, opened the door, and they walked into her bedroom. She stopped, then frowned up at him.

"What? Changing your mind? I can leave, Scarlett. I'd never pressure you."

"Oh, no. I haven't changed my mind. I just realized how small my bed is. You, Noah Conway, are a big man."

He grinned. "Have you heard rumors about me?"

She swatted at him. "No. It's just that it's a queen size, and I'm sure you have a king, don't you?"

"Yes, but we'll make the best of this one. Maybe we can try mine out next time." *What?* He never took women to his place, but looking at her, he could change his mind.

31

"I'd like that, Noah."

"Anytime, darlin'."

"Can I get you anything?" she asked him as she reached up, removed his hat, and tossed it onto the sofa.

"Just you," he said before leaning down and pressing his lips to hers again.

When she leaned her body into his, he wrapped his arms around her and pulled her against him. He walked her backward until she came up against the edge of the bed, then he picked her up and placed her in the center of it. He lay down beside her and pressed his lips to hers. He would never get enough of her lips, and he wanted to feel them on him. Everywhere.

****

She raked her fingers through his thick dark hair and loved the softness of it. She moaned when he moved his lips across her cheek to her earlobe, tugged on it with his teeth, and then slid them down her neck.

"Noah," she whispered.

He raised his head and looked down at her.

"Tell me what you want, baby. I'll do whatever you want," he whispered, then pressed his lips to hers again.

Scarlett moved her hands down from his hair to his broad shoulders, and slid them down his chest and lower to the buckle of his belt and unhooked it, unsnapped his jeans, slowly lowered the zipper, moved her hand inside, and wrapped her fingers around him. She pulled back from him and stared into his beautiful eyes.

"You *are* a big man, Noah Conway," she said with a grin.

32

"Tell me what you want, Scarlett," he repeated.

"You, I want you."

"Not good enough. Tell me."

"Noah Conway, I want you to make me scream," she said, then laughed when he groaned.

He pulled back from her, unsnapped her jeans, moved his hand to the bottom of her T-shirt, and rolled it up to expose her white lace demi-cup bra. Then he ran the tip of his finger over the top of her breast.

"You are so fucking beautiful, Scarlett," he said as he unhooked the front clasp of her bra then moved the cups aside to reveal her breasts. "So beautiful." He leaned down and put his mouth over her nipple, and sucked.

Scarlett grabbed fistfuls of his hair as he sucked on one nipple and ran the pad of his thumb over the other then, he switched as he moved his hand under her jeans to the elastic of her panties. When he moved his finger along the top of them, she arched against his hand.

"Tell me," he said against her breast.

"Touch me, Noah, please," she whimpered.

"Yes, ma'am," he said and dipped his fingers inside her panties to her curls, then he slid one finger down her slit and back up. Over and over.

"Noah," she moaned.

"You're wet, baby."

"I need you inside me. Now."

Noah sat up, and she watched him put his finger in his mouth and suck on it. It was the hottest thing she'd ever seen. He got to his feet, walked to the end of the bed, pulled her boots

33

and socks off, then leaned over and tugged off her jeans.

She sat up, removed her T-shirt and bra then stared at him as he stood at the end of the bed. All she wore was her white bikini panties. She hooked her fingers in the elastic and shoved them down her legs. He pulled them off, dropped them to the floor, all the while keeping his eyes on her, and grinned.

"It is natural," he said, making her laugh.

Scarlett got to her knees, crawled to the bottom of the bed, hooked her fingers in his belt, and pulled him closer. She shoved his jeans down, but he stepped back and turned to sit on the edge of the bed. She watched him remove his boots and socks, then he stood and turned to face her.

"Finish what you started," he told her.

"With pleasure." She pulled him close again, and she could see his hard cock straining the material of his black boxer briefs. She would love to thank the person who invented them because she thought they were the sexiest underwear a man could wear, and Noah Conway proved her point.

He stepped out of his jeans, pulled his T-shirt off, and she hooked her fingers in the elastic band of his boxer briefs and shoved them down. His cock stuck out. Scarlett leaned forward and slid her mouth over the head. Noah's hands gripped her hair, and he thrust his hips but then stepped back from her.

"As much as I would love to have you do that, I need to be inside you," he said and gave her a little shove, so she landed on her back, then he wrapped his hands around her ankles and pulled her to the end of the bed.

"Noah, please, I need you inside me." She needed this man so much.

"I need a condom," he groaned out, then bent over to where his jeans lay, took a condom from his wallet, and sheathed himself. He leaned over her then guided himself in...slow.

She thrust her hips up, and he slammed into her, making her gasp.

"Did I hurt you?" he asked her.

"No. No, you didn't. God, you feel so good. Fuck me." She wrapped her legs around his waist.

"Not as good as you feel, baby." He withdrew and slammed into her hard.

Over and over, he took her close to the edge but wouldn't let her fall.

"Noah, please," she begged. She *needed* that orgasm.

He leaned over her and put his lips just above hers.

"I said I'd do whatever you wanted," he said as he put his hand between them and touched her clitoris, sending her over.

Scarlett screamed, and she had never screamed during sex before, but somehow, she knew this man could make her. He pressed his lips to hers and groaned into her mouth when he came. That was another thing, she never felt a man throb inside of her when he came, but she could feel Noah.

****

Noah raised his head and looked down at her. Her face was flushed, and she was breathing

35

hard. Son of a bitch! Sex had never been that good. *Ever.* He gently pulled out of her, then fell to the bed on his stomach and tried to catch his breath.

He could feel her hand on his sweat-slicked back, so he turned his head to look at her. She smiled at him, making him smile back.

"Hell, that was good," he said between breaths.

"Good is an understatement." Scarlett started to roll to her side but stopped. "I don't think I can move."

Noah chuckled. "We might have to sleep right here."

She laughed. "I'm all for that."

"Shit, I have to get up. I need to get rid of this condom." He rolled to his back, sat up, got to his feet, and then made his way to the bathroom.

After removing the condom, he washed his hands and stared at himself in the mirror. Holy hell. He already wanted her again. As he looked at his reflection, he shook his head. He could see another fucking heartache coming.

Taking a deep breath, he entered the bedroom and chuckled when he saw that she hadn't moved.

"You do plan on staying there, don't you?" He folded his arms and leaned against the doorjamb.

Scarlett raised her head and looked at him.

"Noah Conway, you have one hell of a body," she said, then dropped her head back onto the bed.

He pushed off the doorjamb, walked to the bed, and lifted her. He pulled the covers back and placed her back on the bed, but with her head on the pillow. He crawled in beside her, rolled to his side, and tugged her against him.

"You're staying, right?"

"Yep, unless you want me to go."

"I want you to stay. You do have more condoms, right?"

Noah groaned. "I have one more, but the men's room downstairs has a machine." He chuckled when she burst out laughing.

"Don't go down there naked. There are cameras everywhere."

"Darlin', I have nothing to hide."

"You sure don't, Noah. Not only are you hung, but you also know how to use it."

"Aww, thanks, darlin'," he said, then yawned.

"How did you get this six-pack stomach?" She ran her hand down his abs.

"I work the ranch. Baling hay is one hell of a workout."

She ran her fingertip over his tribal art tattoo covering his right pec and down over his bicep.

"I like this tattoo," she said. "It's sexy."

"I've had it forever." He raised his head and looked at the clock on the bedside table. "It's three in the morning. I need to get some sleep. I have two saddles to work on tomorrow or, rather, today."

"Saddles?"

"I make saddles for a living."

Scarlett sat up. "I didn't know that."

"How could you?"

"Well, I could have asked you what you did. I just never thought about it."

"It's all right, Scarlett. We'll get to know each

other better. I can promise you that."

"Looking forward to it, cowboy." She lay back down and placed her cheek on his chest.

He could get used to this, but he knew not to. She'd leave him too. Of that, he had no doubt.

The next day, he stood in his barn, working on a saddle, but Scarlett kept invading his thoughts. He knew he was going to get in too deep with her. But the sex had never been better, and that just scared the ever-loving hell out of him.

Noah straightened up, arched his back, and groaned as his bones cracked. He walked around the saddle to look it over. It was beautiful, and it had taken him four months to get it right. He'd gone all out on the stitching for this one, but it was how the client wanted it, so Noah always did his best to make it that way.

About the only part of the saddle that didn't have stitching was the seat. The client's name was stitched on the cantle. Some customers wanted a metal plate with their name, but some wanted it stitched there. Noah had no problem doing either. It's what he did, and it was why his saddles sold a lot.

He not only made them specifically for a client, but he also shipped them to retail stores, along with latigo straps and reins. When he started doing this, he never dreamed it would take off as well as it had. He had more than enough money in the bank to live on for the rest of his life and not do a thing, but that wasn't him. He had to keep busy. He walked to the sink, washed his hands, and decided to call Scarlett. He wanted to see her again.

Taking his cellphone from his jeans' back pocket, he scrolled through until he found Scarlett's number and hit *Send*.

"Hey, you," she said when she answered.

"Hey, darlin'. Are you busy?"

"Never too busy for you. What's up?"

"*I* could be..." He grinned when she burst out laughing. "I was calling to see if you wanted to come here for dinner tonight. Since the bar is closed."

"I'd love to. What time?"

"Six?"

"Sounds good. Send me your address, please."

"All right. I'll see you later, Scarlett. Plan on breakfast, too," he said.

"I like pancakes," she said, then disconnected.

He grinned as he put his phone back into his pocket. The day couldn't go fast enough.

****

Scarlett smiled as she placed her cellphone on the coffee table. She couldn't wait to see him again. He was fantastic in bed, and not only that, but he was also a good man. She could see herself falling for him. It had been a while since she'd been this interested in a man. She had told Laura that she wasn't ready to settle down right now, but her and Noah's chemistry had her thinking differently.

She worried her bottom lip as she thought about how she could end up with a broken heart. What had happened that three engagements were called off? She made up her mind that they would talk about that tonight. She wanted to know all about Noah Conway.

At six, she pulled onto a driveway and followed

it to a one-story log home. She had always loved log homes. As she pulled up to the front of the house, she glanced around to see three barns across the yard, about fifty yards away. She smiled when she saw the horses grazing in the corral.

Looking back to the house, she loved the porch going across the front and down the side, she could see. She wondered if it wrapped around the house. After putting the gear into Park, she stepped out.

"Hey."

Scarlett turned to see Noah walking from around the side of the porch.

"Hi," she said with a smile and watched him fold his arms and lean against one of the porch posts. "Your home is beautiful."

"Thanks. Come on in, and I'll show you around."

"Let me get my overnight bag." She opened the back door on her vehicle, pulled the little case out, walked up the steps, and then stopped in front of him. She looked up into that handsome face to see him staring down at her.

Noah leaned down, kissed her lips, then took the case from her and took her hand. He led her to an open door and jerked his chin for her to go inside. She entered and let out a gasp at the kitchen. The exterior walls were log, and in the center of the room sat an island with a black marble top and several stools sitting around it. She looked around to see the countertops matched. The cabinets matched the color of the logs, but the doors were panes of glass. The stove sat within a nook with windows on each side. A large window sat above the sink. She looked up to see the ceiling rose to a point with large logs across it. Looking down, she saw the floor was beige ceramic tile. The dishwasher and refrigerator had wood on them, matching the walls. She noticed a doorway at the end of the counter next to the stove. Walking to it, she peered in to see the laundry room. She turned to look at Noah.

"It's so beautiful. Did you build this home?"

"No, ma'am. I bought it, but I did have a lot of renovations done. The kitchen, living room, and my bedroom."

"I can't wait to see the rest of it."

"Well, come on then." He reached for her hand again and led her into a dining area.

She stopped to admire the room. It was big enough for the table and chairs, and a fireplace sat on the outside wall. Two sets of patio doors looked out onto the porch, one set beside the fireplace.

"Does the porch go all the way around?"

"Yeah, I did add that too."

"Show me more," she said.

Noah grinned. "Follow me."

She walked behind him and had a hard time keeping her eyes off his ass in those tight Wranglers. Damn, the man could fill them out. He stopped inside a room, and she peered around him then gasped again. The entire wall in front of her was two large windows with smaller ones above them. They rose to the ceiling at a point. There were wood trusses across the ceiling. A huge stone fireplace sat against the wall with a big elk head hanging above it to her

41

right. To the left of the hearth sat a flatscreen TV. A dark blue sofa sat facing the fireplace with an overstuffed matching chair on one side of the couch and a recliner on the other. She looked to the left to see more windows and a door with frosted glass. A window with a seat under it sat beside the door. She spun around to look at Noah.

"I love this house."

"Thank you. Let me put this in the bedroom." He started down a hallway beside the fireplace.

"Can I see the bedroom?"

"Of course, come on."

With a smile, she followed him down the hall.

"How many bedrooms?"

"Four, along with an office, five and a half baths."

Scarlett followed him into a room, and her mouth dropped open. The four-poster cherry bed was huge, just as she had figured it would be for him. On the wall across from the foot of the bed sat another stone fireplace with a flatscreen TV above the mantle. A row of windows sat on the outside wall with French doors centered between them. She walked to a doorway and peered in to see the bathroom. The tub was a big jacuzzi surrounded by stone, and the shower took up the back wall. The front was glass with a door centered between a panel on each side, and the three walls were ceramic tile. She could see that a shower head was on each sidewall.

"This bathroom is bigger than my entire apartment."

"I like to get in that jacuzzi after working on saddles all day. There's also a hot tub outside the door in the bedroom I use if I just grab a shower. I get a kink in my back from being on my feet all day." He set her case down inside the door, folded his arms, and leaned against the jamb. "Are you hungry?"

"Starving. What are we having?"

"I thawed some steaks, and I have potatoes ready to nuke."

She kept her eyes on him, but he never moved away from the doorway, so she strode to him and stared up into his eyes.

"Kiss me," she whispered and watched a slow grin lift his lips.

"Yes, ma'am," he said, leaned down, and pressed his lips to hers.

He slid his tongue inside when she opened to him then picked her up. She wrapped her legs around his waist and her arms around his neck. He slowly lifted his lips from hers.

"God, what you do to me, Scarlett," he whispered before taking her lips in a deep hard kiss.

She raked her fingers through his thick hair and moved her tongue against his, making him groan. She pulled her lips from his.

"I feel the same, Noah. Last night was amazing."

"I hope there will be a lot more of them, sweetheart."

"So do I."

He set her on her feet, took her hand, and led her back to the living room.

"Have a seat, and I'll start dinner. My two dogs are out with the men getting some horses in, but they'll be in soon. You're not afraid of dogs, are you?"

"No, I love dogs."

Noah grinned at her. "Good. They'll be all over you."

No sooner had he said that two dogs came running into the room right after she heard a noise in the kitchen. The dogs ran straight to her and sat down. Scarlett laughed.

"Aren't you two just precious?" She squatted down to hug them.

"Don't tell them that."

"What are their names?"

"Sparky and Spike. Sparky is the one with black ears."

"Hi, boys," she said with a laugh and looked up to see Noah rolling his eyes. "How did they get in?"

"There's a pet door in the laundry room. I'll start dinner. Make yourself at home." He turned to leave the room.

"Can I come to the kitchen with you?"

Noah spun around. "Of course, you can. I just thought you'd want to be comfortable."

"I'd rather be with you," she said quietly.

Noah strode to her, leaned down, and kissed her.

"I'd like that too. We can relax after we eat. Come on."

She followed him to the kitchen and took a seat on one of the stools at the island.

"How did you get started making saddles?" She watched as he yanked on the fridge door and removed the steaks.

"I've been doing it since I was sixteen—"

"That long?" she said, then laughed when he

narrowed his eyes at her.

"Yeah, smartass, that long. It all started when I was working on a ranch, and I was not too fond of the saddle I was provided with, so I looked into making one. The rest is history."

"You make them by hand?"

"Yes, one saddle takes me about three months to complete." He shrugged. "Sometimes longer. It depends on how fancy the customer wants it. If they want a lot of stitching, it will take me up to six months. I only make western saddles, though. I've had people come to me for English saddles, but I'm too busy with the other ones to fit those in."

"Do you ever have someone who doesn't like the saddle you made for them?"

"Yes."

"What do you do?"

"They signed a contract, and they have to pay for it. Unless I can sell it, they're responsible for my time and effort."

"Have there been some you couldn't sell?"

He grinned. "Nope."

"That's fascinating. Do you do the work here on your ranch?"

"I have one barn that is used for nothing but saddle making. All the equipment I need is in there. I'm also a guide for elk and mule deer hunts in Kalispell. I own twelve hundred acres there. I have two other guides who work for me. I take time off in November to do several guides."

"You're a busy man," she said.

"I am, but I love it." He shrugged.

Scarlett could tell he loved what he did, but she needed to know why he went through three

45

engagements without making it to the altar.

Chapter Three

Noah wondered if she thought he was *too* busy. It wouldn't be the first time a woman told him that. It was what had ended his relationships in the past. He knew he needed to tell Scarlett about that, too, because he wanted her to know that he would not get married no matter how hot it was between them. Never again would he let a woman into his heart only to have her leave him when he didn't spend enough time with her or give her his undivided attention. At one time, he wanted nothing more than to get married and have a few kids to pass his skills down to, but after three broken engagements, how could he put his heart out there again?

"What are you thinking, Noah?" she asked him.

He glanced over his shoulder and then back to the steaks.

"Nothing."

"If you say so, but you've gone quiet."

Huffing out a sigh, he turned to look at her and wondered how she would take what he had to say.

"Scarlett, I like you. I like being with you, but I have to tell you that I will never get married. I've been engaged three times, and *they* broke the engagements, not me. I wasn't spending enough time with them, so they found someone who would." He stared at her.

"Did I ask you to marry me, Noah Conway?"

"No, ma'am, but I don't want you to—"

"To what? Hear wedding bells? We just got together, Noah. I'm not ready for any of that either."

"But I'm *never* going to be ready for it, Scarlett. I can't go through it again. I hate even to admit it, but if I fell for you and you left me, I think it would hurt me a lot worse than the other three times. I can't chance it." He shook his head and folded his arms. "So if you're looking for more, then maybe we should just stop this now."

"I'm fine, Noah. I just bought the bar, so I'm not looking for anything permanent either."

He raised his eyebrow. "Sure?"

"Yep. Now, make me some dinner. I'm hungry."

"Yes, ma'am." He winked, then turned to get the steaks placed on the broiler pan, and then he slid them into the oven. "How do you like your steak?"

"Medium rare, please."

"Good. They won't take long then. It's how I like mine too."

Noah was relieved that she didn't want anything permanent. Maybe this time, he'd be able to walk away with his heart still intact.

"Who were they, Noah? The women who hurt you?"

He strolled to the island and took a seat on one of the stools.

"First was Joanna. I met her right after high school. I worked on her parent's ranch. We fell in love. I was getting a lot of orders for my saddles, and of course, I didn't spend enough time with her. She broke the engagement six months after

48

I put that ring on her finger. Looking back, I know it was probably for the best. We were young." He shrugged. "Then, when I was twenty-five, I met Leigh, and I fell for her. We were together for two years, and then we got engaged. She even started planning the wedding, but again, I worked too much. At that time, I had started the hunting trips too, so the more I was gone, the angrier she got. The wedding was called off a month before it was to happen. I had just about given up on ever getting married. I wanted to. I did. I wanted to have kids, so when I met Vicki, I was sure she was the one. I fell hard for her. I met her when her father wanted a saddle made, and she came with him. I think I fell for her the minute I laid eyes on her. She felt the same. At least, she said she did. She moved in with me, and I put a ring on her finger too. We were together for two years, but we got into it big time when I had to fill in for one of my guides. He was down with the flu, and there was no one else. Vicki and I were to go away that week, and I had to cancel. Those hunters pay a lot of money for those trips, so I had no choice. She told me it was either I go away with her or go on the hunting trip. I told her I had to go and she didn't say anything more about it, but when I came home, she was gone. The ring was on the nightstand, along with a note telling me that no woman would put up with this. That was three years ago. I stay away from relationships now because it will end up the same. I'm either in the barn making saddles, running the ranch, or on hunting trips. I suppose no woman likes being alone that much."

He got down from the stool, walked to the oven, picked up a potholder, opened the door, and flipped the steaks. He put two potatoes in the microwave, set the timer then got back on the stool. Scarlett sat there, staring at him. He raised his eyebrow at her.

"I'm sure some women don't like being alone a lot, but I would think when you are with someone you love, you take advantage of it. Those women sound a little selfish to me. I like my alone time." She shrugged.

"Yeah, well, all three of them said the same thing when I told them how busy I was. They didn't realize they'd be alone so much."

"No matter who I end up with, that man will have to know that about me too. I'm so busy with the bar. I'm open every day except Sunday. I might not open until four, but I'm still busy. I have to do inventory, stock the bar, place orders, and so on. The man I marry will have to see that, or it won't work."

Noah nodded then got off the stool when the microwave dinged. He took the potatoes out, put them on plates, pulled the steaks out of the oven, and placed them on the plates. He carried them to the island and set a plate in front of her.

"Let me grab the stuff for the potatoes, and then we can eat."

"All right." She smiled up at him.

He grinned at her. After getting everything for the potatoes, he resumed his seat at the bar, and they began to eat.

"This steak is so good," Scarlett said after she chewed and swallowed a piece of it.

"It is good. I usually buy a side of beef from

50

either Preston Mitchell or Calder Moore. Both have great cattle beef. They raise Angus."

"They're both nice men."

"They're good friends of mine. We've known each other since grade school."

"Really? Who else?"

Noah cut into his steak. "Reece Maddox, Boone Evans, Dominic Blackstone, Wilder Richards, Landry Yates, Rand Morris, Creed McBride, and Grant Hunter. I have friends I've known practically all my life here and in Spring City and Hartland. Some are older, and some are younger. All three are tight-knit communities."

"I cannot believe that Grant Hunter lives here in Clifton."

"He's a great guy. Did you know he owns the Hartland Restaurant?"

"Yes. Laura told me about that. He came in the bar one night, and I was fangirling all over him."

Noah chuckled. "Probably not as bad as Sloane did when she met him."

"Sloane? She owns the bakery, right?"

"Yes, a hell of a baker. She's married to Holt James, another good friend of mine. He's a little older than me, but I've known him for years. Seems Holt took her to dinner one night in Hartland when they were dating, and Grant was there. Holt said Sloane could hardly speak." Noah chuckled.

Scarlett laughed. "I bet all of you think it's crazy how women go nuts over him."

Noah shrugged. "We all had a feeling Grant would make it big. Hell, he could sing when he was in elementary school, and once that bug bit him, he knew he was going to head for Nashville. He made it, but he's happy to be home. He loves running the ranch, and he's incredibly happy with Jessa."

"I met her too. She is so sweet." Scarlett put her knife and fork down. "I haven't seen Calder in the bar lately. He used to stop in once in a while."

"He's married now."

"Really? I didn't know that."

"Yep, to Jessa's best friend, Mitzie Patterson. Mitzie came here from Nashville to get over a broken engagement and got stranded in the snow." Noah chuckled. "Calder came along and rescued her. It was touch and go for a while because she wasn't sure she wanted to move here, but they fell in love. I'm glad he's finally met someone. Besides Trick, he's about the only one of us who wanted to settle down and get married. Hell, he had women after him all the damn time."

"He's gorgeous, so that I can understand. Those eyes," Scarlett said with a sigh.

Noah cleared his throat, making her look at him. He narrowed his eyes when she winked at him and reached her hand out to touch his cheek.

"You're gorgeous too, Noah. I thought so the first time I saw you. Your eyes are amazing."

He leaned over and gave her a quick kiss.

"Good save." He chuckled when she burst out laughing.

After dinner, they cleaned up the kitchen, and Noah made them each a cup of coffee. Then they headed for the living room. The dogs were lying in front of the fireplace. He watched as Scarlett took a seat on the sofa and curled her legs under her.

"Can you make a fire?"

"I can if you want one."

"I would love one, Noah," she said.

"I told you last night, I'd do anything you wanted." He set his cup on the coffee table, walked to the fireplace, reached up and opened the flue, then struck a match to the wood. He straightened up and stared into the flames as they wrapped around the wood.

"That smells so good," Scarlett said.

Noah turned around, strode back to the sofa, and took a seat beside her.

"I love the smell of the wood burning."

"Is the fireplace in the bedroom woodburning too?"

"No, it's natural gas. We get some harsh winters here, so there is always a chance the power can go out. If it does, I stay in the bedroom because I don't feel like freezing my balls off to go outside and get wood."

Scarlett burst out laughing. "I get that."

Noah looked over at her with a grin. "I have some stacked on the back porch for this one, but I'd run out of wood too quick if I had to keep both of them going."

Their eyes met and held. He watched as she set her cup on the table, then she leaned forward and kissed his lips. He cupped her face in his hands and deepened the kiss.

"I think I'd like to see the bedroom again," she whispered against his lips.

Noah shot to his feet, picked her up, and carried her to his bedroom. He kicked the door closed, then made his way to the bed and placed her in its center. He straightened up, tugged off his T-shirt, and toed off his boots. He kept his eyes on her as she watched him. When he reached for the snap of his jeans, she got to her knees, crawled to him, unsnapped them, and lowered the zipper with a sharp tug. He hissed in a breath.

"Christ, I'm glad you didn't catch something in that zipper."

She looked up at him. "I would have kissed it and made it feel better."

"I'm so fucking hard for you," he murmured.

"I want you so much, Noah." She pulled her T-shirt off, kicked off her shoes, and removed her jeans.

He swore he came a little when he saw the black lace bra and matching panties. Son of a bitch. If he didn't have her soon, it would be over before it even got started.

When she pushed his jeans and boxer briefs down, his dick jutted out. He kept his eyes on her as she leaned forward and slid her mouth down over him. *Hell!* He wanted this, but he also wanted to fuck her. Her hand wrapped around the base of his cock, and she pumped it as she continued to suck on him.

Noah stepped back, gave her a little shove to make her fall onto her back, then he wrapped his hands around her ankles, tugged her to the edge of the bed, and he went to his knees. He placed his thumbs on each side of her slit, pulled it apart, then placed his mouth over her clitoris. Then he kissed her thigh and ran his tongue across the top of her curls. He could smell her arousal, and he was so fucking hard, he didn't think he'd ever be soft again. Her gasp filled the room.

Had a woman ever tasted better? Not to him. He moved his tongue down her slit and back up and sucked on her again. Her breathing got heavier, and he knew she was close. Her hands fisted in his hair just as she cried out his name. He opened the nightstand drawer, removed a condom, quickly sheathed himself, and thrust hard into her. He leaned over her, pressed his lips to hers, then hovered them above hers.

"Let's do that again," he said before pressing his lips to hers as he began to slide in and out of her. Her legs wrapped around his waist and her hands clutched his hair. He pulled his lips from hers and stared into her face. She had her eyes closed. "Look at me."

Scarlett opened her eyes and stared up at him. He never took his eyes from hers as she tumbled over again. She put her fist over her mouth as she screamed. Noah slammed into her harder as his belly clenched, and he knew he was going over. He groaned as he came hard.

****

Scarlett lowered her legs from around his waist, and they felt like rubber. Damn, it was hot with this man. She couldn't see another man ever satisfying her as Noah could. He collapsed onto the bed beside her. She looked over at him to see his chest heaving, and she touched his arm.

"Next time, how about I do some of the work?"

Noah chuckled. "I'm fine with that."

He sat up, got up from the bed, and entered

the bathroom. Scarlett couldn't move to save her life. She raised her head when he cleared his throat, and she looked to the door to see him leaning against the doorjamb.

"How about a shower?"

"Sure, if you carry me in there," she said with a laugh.

"I can do that."

She watched him stroll to the bed, then he took her hand, scooped her up into his arms, and carried her into the bathroom.

Later, she jerked awake and wondered what had woken her. She reached out for Noah, but he wasn't in bed. Sitting up, she looked at the clock to see it was close to two. She swung her legs over the side of the bed, got to her feet, and looked for his T-shirt. She found it on the floor, picked it up, pulled it over her head and down her body.

Tiptoeing to the door, she opened it and looked down the hall. She could see a light shining in the living room, so she made her way there.

She came to a halt when she saw him sitting in the recliner, staring at the fire burning in the hearth. She slowly made her way to him and stopped beside his chair. All he had on was a pair of sweatpants. When she touched him, he jerked and looked up at her.

"Why are you up?" he asked her.

"Why are you?"

Noah shrugged. "I couldn't sleep."

"Is something wrong?"

"No."

For some reason, she didn't believe him.

Something was bothering him, but she was too afraid to hear what it was. Was he thinking that he should never have started seeing her? But why? She took a deep breath and knew there was only one way to find out.

"Noah? Are you regretting this?"

He looked up at her with surprise on his face. "No, why would I?"

"I don't know. You just seem a little distant."

"I told you I couldn't sleep. Some nights I just have too much on my mind, and it keeps me awake."

"Like what?" she asked him as she moved to sit on his lap. She sighed when his arms wrapped around her.

"Orders for saddles, mostly. I have a two-year waiting list, and I wonder if it's worth it at times."

"Have you thought of hiring help?"

Noah blew out a laugh. "Then it wouldn't be an original Conway saddle, would it?"

"I suppose not. You shouldn't push yourself so hard. You need time for you."

"That's why I go on the hunting trips in November. It gets me away for a while. I love hunting, and seeing the looks on those hunters' faces when they get that big game is very satisfying."

"Tell me about it."

"Not much to tell. Eight hunters on each trip. It's a five-day minimum for the hunt. There are cabins there for them. Meals are supplied too, and rifles if they don't bring their own."

"Sounds like you go all out for them."

"Well, for what they pay, it's only right."

"Is it expensive?"

"Ten thousand for a week."

"What? I'm sorry, did you say ten...*thousand?* Per person?"

"Yes, ma'am."

"Unreal. I'm in the wrong business."

Noah chuckled. "It's amazing what people will pay to hunt in Montana."

"How do you take them?"

"They have to get themselves to Kalispell, but once we go out, it's on horseback. If anyone gets an animal, I'll call back to the lodge, and the men will come out in the truck, and if need be, hike back to where the animal is. I'll do the field dressing before they get there, then they'll take the animal back to the lodge."

"Field dressing?"

"Yes, it's removing the internal organs, and it's necessary for preserving the meat. It has to be done as soon as possible to ensure rapid body heat loss and prevent bacteria from growing on the surface of the carcass."

She shuddered. "I'm not sure I could do that."

"Has to be done, darlin'."

"Do you eat the meat?"

"Yes, a requirement to hunt with me is that it is for the meat, not a trophy. If they get one they want to be mounted, that's fine, but they have to either take the meat or donate it to people who need it."

"Well, that's good. Did you shoot that one?" She pointed to the one above the mantle.

"I did. That was from last year. There's a mule deer mounted in my office that I got about three years ago."

She placed her cheek on the top of his head.

58

"Come back to bed, Noah."

"All right. I have to get up in a few hours. I have two saddles to work on."

Scarlett got to her feet, put her hand out to him then pulled him up from the chair. She led him back to the bedroom. He started to remove his sweatpants, but she pushed his hands away, hooked her fingers in the elastic, and shoved them down to his feet. He stepped out of them and kept his eyes on her.

With a smile, she got to her knees, leaned forward, and kissed the head of his dick. His hands thrust into her hair as he groaned. His dick rose as she sucked on him. She pulled back and looked up at him.

"Sit down," she said.

Noah sat on the edge of the bed while their eyes held. She didn't take her eyes off him as she leaned down and took him into her mouth again. His hands clutched her hair then smoothed over it.

Scarlett wrapped one hand around his hard cock and kneaded his balls with the other. She kept at it until he tried to pull back from her.

"Scarlett, baby, you have to stop," he groaned out.

"Nope. You have taken me over like this. I'm returning the favor," she said, then slid her mouth down over him again and sucked hard. He hardened more, then a low groan tore from him as he came, and he fell back onto the bed.

She kissed her way up his body to his lips and pressed hers to his. She raised her lips from his and looked down into his face. He opened his eyes and stared into hers.

"You didn't have to do that," he said between breaths.

"I know. I wanted to. I believe it's give and take in sex." She quickly kissed his lips. "All sex. I've been with men who have wanted me to do it, but they never wanted to return the favor. Women like oral sex too."

"I'll be happy to let you do that anytime," he said, then chuckled.

"And I'll be happy to let you return the favor. You are an amazing man, Noah. Both in bed and out. Now let's get some sleep. I think you're supposed to make me pancakes for breakfast."

"Yes, ma'am. By the way, I like seeing you in my shirt."

She got to her feet, walked around the bed, pulled the T-shirt off, and crawled in. He rolled to face her then tugged her close. It wasn't long before she heard his deep, even breathing and knew he had fallen asleep. She still thought something was wrong, but she wasn't going to pressure him to tell her what it was.

****

Noah worked in the barn on a saddle a week later, but his mind was on Scarlett. He should just break it off with her now. She might say she doesn't want to get married, but most women do, and he'd bet money that she was one of them. Maybe not right now, but soon.

"Shit," he muttered.

He knew he shouldn't have gotten involved with her. Just after being with her a couple of times had him thinking in ways he shouldn't. He did not want to go through it again. He was tired of putting his heart out there, only to be told he

60

worked too much. He had two businesses to run, plus the ranch. How the hell did anyone expect him to stop and be with them all the damn time?

He was too busy. That was all he ever heard. Three engagements, three called off. No weddings. He had wanted children so he could teach them his skills. So they'd take over when he was gone. Was it too much to ask?

"Hey, boss."

Noah looked to the door to see Brad, his ranch manager, enter.

"What's up?"

"When was the last time you looked outside?" Brad asked him with a grin.

"Not since I came in here about two hours ago. Why?"

"It's snowing. We're going to get the horses in."

"Is it snowing that bad?"

"Hell, yeah. We have about three inches already, and it's still coming down. You can barely see the house from here."

"No shit?" Noah picked up a rag, wiped his hands, and walked out into the barn's aisle to the doors. He slid one open, and his jaw dropped. "Damn."

"It wasn't even calling for snow today, but we know how that goes."

"Hell, yes. Get the men up there and get those horses. I'm going to finish the saddle I'm working on and call it a day. Send the men home too."

"Will do."

Noah watched as Brad stepped out into the snow then disappeared. He shook his head as he slid the door closed then headed back to the workshop. He only had one saddle to finish today, and then he would relax. See? He could take time off if he wanted. Shaking his head, he reentered the room and got back to work.

Later, as he sat in the recliner, he stared at his cellphone lying on the arm of it. With a heavy sigh, he picked it up and called Scarlett.

"Hey, cowboy," she said in a soft voice, and his damn dick betrayed him.

"Hey, darlin', are you at the bar?"

"I am, but it's dead. I suppose the snow kept everyone home. Are you in where it's warm?"

"I'm in the house. As for being warm, I'd be a lot warmer if you were here."

Her laughter came over the line, making him grin.

"I wish I could be there too, but I don't drive in this stuff."

"No one should be out tonight. I just wanted to see if you were okay."

"I'm fine. I think I'm just going to close and go upstairs. I'll take a nice hot bath and relax."

"Sounds good, darlin'. I'll talk to you tomorrow."

"I'll be waiting," she whispered and disconnected.

"Son of a bitch," he swore. "You just told yourself that you should break it off with her. All she has to do is talk to you, and your fucking dick goes rock hard. You fucking dumbass."

He lifted the footrest, closed his eyes, and tried to convince himself that it was best to stay the hell away from her. She already had him feeling things he shouldn't. He also knew she suspected something was up last week when she found him in the living room. Having her beside him felt...right, and he couldn't let it. He hadn't even slept an hour when he got up.

She was so damn hot, though, and he doubted he'd find that with another woman. What the hell was he supposed to do? He couldn't make her any promises, but he couldn't stay away from her either.

****

Scarlett placed her cellphone on the bar and stared at it. Something wasn't right. She loved that he had called, but she still sensed a distance. Since last week, he has been different toward her. Did she imagine things?

She jerked when the door opened, and she looked over to see the cowboys who had started trouble with Noah enter. She straightened up to watch them stroll in and take seats at the bar. It was just them and her, and she didn't like it one bit.

"Bad weather to be out in, boys," she said as she moved to where they sat.

"It's never too bad out to be in a bar," Jayden Powers said with a grin.

Scarlett gave a tightlipped smile. "Well, what can I get you? You'll have to make it quick since I plan on closing in a few minutes."

Powers leaned back, put his hand over his heart, and widened his eyes.

"Come on now, sugar, we're paying customers," he said as he glanced around then looked back to her. "Where's your badass boyfriend?"

"Upstairs. Waiting for me," she said. There was no way she'd let them know she was alone.

"I see. He lets you down here alone?"

"I told him I was coming down to lock up." She tilted her head. "Now, what can I get you?"

Placing his hands on the bar, Powers got to his feet.

"Never mind, sugar, we'll go."

"All right. You be careful out there," Scarlett said but didn't move to follow them to the doors. She was too damn scared, but she would never let them see it.

"We will."

They started toward the door, but Powers stopped, turned around, grinned, and touched the brim of his hat.

"We'll be back, though. You can count on that." He turned back around and strode out the door with the other men.

Scarlett blew out a relieved breath, then quickly made her way around the bar to the door, locked it, and looked out the window in the door to see them all getting into a black pickup truck, and then they drove off. She turned, leaned her back against the door, and tried to calm herself down. They were up to something, and it terrified her.

After ensuring everything was off and locked up, she climbed the stairs to her apartment. She stopped halfway up, turned to make sure the door closed and locked before continuing to the top. She unlocked her door, stepped inside then locked it behind her. For the first time since living alone, she was scared.

Scarlett stood behind the bar a few weeks later, mentally shaking her head. It was crazy tonight. There'd already been three fights the bouncers had to break up. All the guys were warned one more time, and they were banned from the bar. Why did men think fists were the best way to settle an argument? What happened to just having your own opinion without someone getting punched?

She turned to a good-looking cowboy, who took a seat on a stool and walked to him with a frustrated sigh.

"What can I get you?" she asked.

"Beer is fine, ma'am. Whatever's on tap. I'm not picky," he said with a grin.

"I wish they were all as easy as you." She laughed.

He looked up at her and widened his eyes. "I'm easy?" He shook his head. "Damn, I've never been called easy."

Scarlett laughed and turned away to get his beer. As she held the glass under the spout, she pulled the lever and watched the beer fill it, making sure to keep the foam at a minimum. When she turned to set it in front of him, she saw Jeb Carson taking a seat at the bar and shook her head. He just couldn't let Laura out of his sight. He had it bad, she thought with a smile. She watched him smile, and she glanced around to look for Laura because Scarlett was sure the woman would have a big smile on her face seeing Jeb here, but she didn't see her.

Scarlett frowned when she saw Marie smiling back at Jeb. She shook her head. Jeb was probably just being nice, but something was nagging at her. With a sigh, she was sure she imagined things. Jeb loved Laura. They'd been married quite a few years and were happy. At least, she thought they were.

She turned when she saw Laura spot Jeb and head for him. She leaned over the bar and kissed him, and everyone along the bar cheered. Yeah, Scarlett was sure she just imagined things. But her gut was usually right. She glanced around to look for Marie and spotted her staring at Jeb and Laura with a frown on her face. Scarlett took a deep breath and walked to Jeb when Laura moved on to a customer.

"Hey, Jeb."

"Hi, Scarlett. How are you tonight?"

"I'm good." She leaned against the bar. "You just can't stay away from her, can you?"

"Laura?"

Scarlett straightened up. *What a strange response.*

"Who else would I mean, Jeb?"

He laughed, and for some reason, it grated on her nerves.

"I'm teasing. Of course, Laura. I like watching her work," he said with a grin, and Scarlett wanted to throat punch him.

"I know you like watching...her," she said and turned away from him.

Something was not right here, but until she was sure, she would never say anything to Laura. Call it women's intuition or whatever, Scarlett didn't think Jeb was on the up and up about why he was here when Laura was. Scarlett turned back around to look at him.

Jeb raised his beer bottle to his lips and took a long swig. He set the bottle down, spun around on the stool, and watched the people on the dance floor. Scarlett wasn't sure about that either because Marie was in his line of sight serving patrons. *Damn it. Do not make assumptions, Scarlett.*

As the night wore on, she had gotten to the point where she was sure she had imagined things. Laura would walk over to Jeb, kiss him and get back to work. Scarlett shook her head. She was just glad she'd never said anything to Laura. She was sure that would end a good friendship.

"Don't stick your nose where it doesn't belong," she muttered.

"Did you say something?"

Scarlett glanced over to see Laura standing beside her, making a drink.

"Talking to myself. Nothing new," Scarlett said with a smile.

"I do that all the time, too," Laura said.

"Laura?"

"Yes?"

"Does it bother you that Jeb is always here when you're working?"

She watched as Laura set the drink down and looked at her.

"Honestly, sometimes I wish he'd just let me do my job without being here. I don't need him here...watching me." Laura shrugged.

"Have you told him that?"

"I did, and he just said he hates being home alone, but he doesn't need to be here all the time." Laura tilted her head. "I feel like he doesn't trust me."

Scarlett's mouth dropped open, and she snapped it shut.

"You would never cheat on him."

"No, I wouldn't." Laura picked up the drink. "I

67

need to get this to the customer."

Scarlett watched her walk to the end of the bar, set the drink down in front of a cowboy then move on to the next one to take an order. Scarlett looked over her shoulder at Jeb, but again, he wasn't looking at Laura. He was watching Marie. *Damn!*

As she set a beer on the bar in front of another cowboy, she glanced toward the door when it opened and grinned when she saw Noah making his way through the crowd. He took a seat on a stool next to Jeb. She watched them talking then made her way to him.

"Noah, what would you like?"

"What a question, Scarlett," he said with a grin.

She laughed.

"To drink," she emphasized.

"Oh, sure. Beer is fine."

"I'll be right back."

"Yes, ma'am." He grinned.

She poured him a beer in a frosted glass, set it down in front of him, and looked at Jeb.

"Another beer, Jeb?"

"No, thanks, Scarlett. I need to keep my wits about me."

"All right. Let me know if you change your mind."

"Yeah, I will," he said while glancing around the bar, making her frown.

Scarlett looked at Noah, but he didn't seem to notice anything amiss. If Jeb was fooling around, it was none of her business, but Laura was her friend. She mentally shook her head.

When the doors opened again, people started

cheering, and she looked over to see...Grant Hunter enter. *Grant Hunter was in her bar again!*

"Are you catching flies?"

She glanced at Noah then back to Grant.

"I can't believe he's in here again."

Noah chuckled. "He enjoys coming in here."

"And Jessa is with him."

"Stop staring at the man," Noah growled out.

Scarlett snorted. "Oh, please. What woman wouldn't stare."

She watched as Grant and Jessa made their way through the crowd and took seats at the bar. She turned away from Noah.

"Hey," Noah said, making her turn back to him.

"Yeah?"

"*Yeah?* You're leaving me for Hunter?"

"Sorry...but, yes." She laughed then made her way to Grant and Jessa. She stepped in front of them. "Hi, you two. What can I get you?"

"Hey, Scarlett. How are you doing?" Grant asked her.

She stared at him and was in awe of how good-looking he was. Those piercing, dark eyes were gorgeous.

"I'm good. Hi, Jessa."

"Hi, Scarlett. Could I get a Callahan and Coke, please?"

"Of course. What about you, Grant?"

"Plain Coke. I'm driving," he said with a wink, and she just about swooned.

"All right. I'll be right back with your drinks."

As the night wore on, it seemed to get more crowded. She never knew how busy the place got. Her uncle had tried to warn her, but she didn't think it was going to be like this. She looked over to Noah to see him still talking with Jeb.

She saw Laura waiting on people lining the bar, but she didn't go back to where Jeb sat. Scarlett glanced around to see where Marie was and saw her serving drinks at the tables. Then she headed back behind the bar and walked up to her.

"Can I take my break?"

Scarlett looked at her watch. "Yes, but don't take longer than your fifteen minutes. I need you back here as soon as possible. We're crazy tonight."

"No problem. I just need some fresh air," Marie told her, set the tray down she'd been holding, walked back the hallway, came back out with her coat, and walked outside.

A minute later, Scarlett turned to see if Noah wanted another beer and saw him sitting alone, so she made her way to him.

"Hey, do you want another?"

"No, I'm good. I'm driving."

"You could just stay here tonight," Scarlett said with a smile on her face.

"Well, in that case, darlin', I'll take another beer."

"All right. Hey, where's Jeb?"

"He said he needed to get some fresh air." Noah shrugged.

Funny, Marie had said the same thing. Scarlett mentally shrugged. So what if they were outside at the same time? It was just a coincidence.

"Coincidence, my ass," she muttered.

"What?" Noah frowned at her.

"Nothing. Just something on my mind." She touched his hand. "I'll be right back with your beer. Don't go anywhere."

"Only upstairs with you later, baby."

"Right, so don't get drunk."

Noah chuckled. "Yes, ma'am."

Scarlett smiled, got him a beer, and kept an eye on the door.

Chapter Four

Noah watched as Scarlett waited on everyone at the bar. Between her and Laura, no one was left without a drink. He raised his glass to Grant and grinned when he saw him say something to Jessa, get down from the stool and head his way.

"Hey, Noah, how goes it?" Grant asked as he took a seat on the stool Jeb had vacated.

"I'm good, Grant. You?"

"Good, thanks. Damn, this place packs them in, doesn't it?"

"Yeah, every weekend, I'm sure." Noah picked up his glass and took a sip of beer.

"You got something going on with Scarlett?"

Noah inhaled and almost choked on the beer. He gave Grant a dirty look when he chuckled.

"Why do you ask that?"

Grant grinned. "Because you haven't taken your eyes off her since I got here."

"Mind your own fucking business, Hunter," Noah growled.

"I'm hurt, Noah."

"Yeah, you are." He turned on the stool to look at his friend. "We've been seeing each other for a while, and that's all you need to know."

"Right." Grant took a drink from his glass.

"How are you and Jessa doing?" Noah watched as Grant looked over to where Jessa sat then back to him.

"Love of my life." Grant shrugged.

"I'm happy for you. It looks like being married

agrees with you."

"It does." Grant got down from the stool. "And when are you going to marry that one?"

Noah started to say something, but Grant walked off. As much as he would love to have Scarlett permanently in his life, it wouldn't happen. He knew she would break it off with him once he hadn't spent enough time with her. Women wanted to spend time with their men, and he didn't provide that enough for any woman.

He also knew, though, for now, he'd spend as much time with her that he could. He couldn't stay away, and he might as well accept that his heart was going to end up broken again. Hell, he should be used to it. Maybe it wouldn't hurt as bad this time. He snorted. He knew it was going to hurt worse. Son of a bitch! He just needed to stay the hell on his ranch, do his work, and keep the hell away from women.

"Yeah, like that will happen," he muttered.

"What?"

Noah looked over to see Jeb getting on the stool beside him and shook his head.

"Nothing. Talking to myself. As usual."

"Woman troubles?" Jeb asked with a chuckle.

"What other kind of trouble do most men have?"

"That's true." Jeb raised his hand to Scarlett.

"What can I get you, Jeb?" Scarlett asked when she got to him.

"Another beer, please."

"Sure. Did you get some fresh air?" Scarlett said, her voice dripping with sarcasm.

Noah glanced between Scarlett and Jeb, then

frowned.

"Uh, yeah. It was just a little stuffy in here," Jeb said.

"A little cold out, though, isn't it?"

"I was in my truck."

"I'll be right back with your beer," Scarlett said and headed for the cooler.

"What the hell was that about?" Noah asked.

"No clue. Who knows how a woman thinks?" Jeb shook his head.

Noah didn't understand why Scarlett talked to Jeb in that manner, but he planned to find out later.

****

Scarlett twisted the cap off the beer, walked to Jeb, and set it on the bar in front of him. When he thanked her, she nodded then turned away to wait on other customers. She knew by the look on Noah's face that he was probably wondering what the hell was wrong with her, and she wasn't sure she'd tell him. He'd probably tell her she imagined things. Yeah, she was telling herself that too, but when Marie came back in right after Jeb had, she was pretty sure she was right.

She glanced around to see where Marie was and saw her serving drinks to people at a table. Marie had no morals. Any woman who would screw around with a married man and work with that man's wife had no morals at all.

Scarlett hated the idea of Laura finding out. *If it's true, you cannot make assumptions!* Sighing, she decided to wait and see. Because if it was true, she knew that Laura would eventually find out. The wife always does. Laura would find out one way or another, but Scarlett also knew she

74

would not be the one to tell her. Unless she actually caught Jeb, she would not tell Laura of her suspicions.

After setting another drink in front of Jessa, she smiled as she watched Grant slide his hand under her hair, touch her neck, lean over and kiss her temple. Scarlett could hear her sigh from across the bar.

"Scarlett, would you mind if I sang with the band?" Grant asked her.

"Oh, my God! Please do. I would love it, and I know the crowd would."

Grant grinned. "All right." He got down from the stool, kissed Jessa's temple again, and strode through the crowd.

Scarlett grinned as she watched him make his way to the stage. It wasn't easy since just about everyone stopped him or reached out to touch him. When he stepped onto the stage, the crowd roared. He picked up an acoustic guitar and started singing one of his best-selling songs. A fast one that got the crowd singing along with him.

"Grant sure got the crowd going, didn't he?" Jessa asked her.

"He's fantastic. I miss hearing him sing, so anytime he wants to while he's here, he is more than welcome."

"I'm sure he'll take you up on that."

Scarlett glanced around and saw Noah raise his hand at her.

"I'll talk to you in a little while, Jessa. I need to get these people their drinks."

"No problem." Jessa turned on the stool to watch Grant sing.

75

"What can I get you, cowboy?" Scarlett asked Noah when she got to him, leaned her arms on the bar, and looked into his eyes.

"For now, a beer."

"Be right back." She picked up his glass, walked to the sink, placed the mug in it, got another frosted mug from the freezer, set it under the tap, filled it, and took it back to him. "You let me know what I can get you later."

"Damn, Scarlett, don't say shit like that."

She laughed. "I love teasing you, Noah Conway."

A grin lifted his sexy lips. "Right back at ya, darlin'."

Straightening up, she glanced at Jeb to see him looking over the crowd and smiling. She looked to see Marie smiling at him. *Damn!*

"Can I get you anything, Jeb?"

"No, I'm good. Thanks, though, Scarlett." He smiled at her, and it took all her willpower not to knock his teeth out.

Scarlett's imagination was in overdrive. As the night wore on, she finally convinced herself that she was wrong about Jeb and Marie. He doted on Laura when she would talk to him.

Finally, she rang the bell and shouted that it was last call. One more hour, and she could go upstairs and have her way with Noah. Nibbling on her lip, she glanced over to where he sat to see him watching her. When he saw her looking his way, he winked at her, making her grin.

An hour later, she locked the doors, turned to see Noah still sitting on the stool, made her way to him, and stepped between his thighs. She leaned forward and pressed her lips to his. His arms wrapped around her, and he lifted her to straddle his lap.

His lips moved across her cheek to her ear, then down to her neck.

"I want you," he whispered.

"I want you too. Let's go upstairs."

He pulled back. "Why? Can't we just do it on the bar?"

She swatted at him, making him laugh.

"Not on my bar, Noah Conway. How sanitary is that?"

"For God's sake, who thinks of that?"

"Someone who owns a bar and has a man who thinks that way."

Noah laughed. "Caught me." He set her on her feet then got to his. "All right, baby, let's go upstairs. Do we need to clean up here first?"

"Nope. Since tomorrow is Sunday, I'll do it then."

He kissed her temple. "I'll help."

"Damn right you will, Noah. Now come on," she said as she took his hand then led him to the door leading to her apartment.

****

Noah let her lead him down the hall to the door and had one hell of a time keeping his eyes off her ass in those damn tight Wranglers. They were just as hot as the short, bibbed overalls she was wearing the night he met her. Shit, his dick was hard already.

After opening the door, she turned to look at him and walked backward up the stairs. He wanted to take her on the damn steps. He couldn't stop the grin as she ran her tongue along her lower lip.

"You're killing me," he said.

"I don't want to do that. I just want to get you to my bed."

He chuckled. "I'm not sure I can make it that far."

Scarlett stopped on the step above him, making them eye-level, and raised an eyebrow.

"No?"

"No promises, darlin'."

"Hmmm, well, maybe we don't have to make it to the bed," she said, and as he watched, she removed her T-shirt, unhooked her bra, dropped them onto the step, and reached for the snap on her jeans.

Before she could unsnap them, he shot into action, pulled her close, and took a nipple into his mouth, and sucked. She took his hat off, dropped it, and raked her fingers through his hair. She shoved his coat off, making it fall to the steps, and reached for the snap on his jeans. When she slowly lowered the zipper, reached in, and wrapped her fingers around him, he knew he had to slow down.

"Scarlett—"

"I need you so much, Noah." She pushed his jeans and boxer briefs down to his knees. She moved back from him and sat on the step. She leaned forward, took his hard cock into her mouth, and sucked on him. Hard. He groaned as he fisted his hands in her hair.

"Scarlett, I need to be inside you. Please, baby."

She toed off her boots, stood, unsnapped her jeans, lowered the zipper, and shimmied out of them, along with her panties, and stared at him.

"Sit down," she told him.

Swallowing hard, Noah turned, sat on the step, and watched her step in front of him. She gave him a sly smile and straddled his lap. His dick stood straight up between them.

"Baby, please," he begged. "Get a condom from my wallet."

She removed his wallet from the back pocket of his jeans, took a condom out, handed it to him. He ripped it open and sheathed himself.

"Beg again, Noah," she whispered next to his ear.

"Damn it, Scarlett. Please, just fucking ride me."

"Anything for you, baby." She stood up then he watched her move her hand down her belly to her curls. When she dipped her finger between her slit, he almost came.

"Fuck, Scarlett, give me a taste."

She laughed, stuck her finger in his mouth, and he sucked on it. God! He loved the taste of this woman. She straddled his lap again and slowly impaled herself on him. He tightened his grip on her hips. She placed her hands on his shoulders and moved up and down his hard length.

Noah moved his hands up to cup her face and took her lips in a deep kiss. He moved one hand down between them to touch her clitoris. He pulled his lips from hers.

"Beg for it, Scarlett. Beg for that orgasm," he murmured against her lips.

"Noah, please. I need that orgasm. Get me there, please," she moaned and moved her face to the crook of his neck.

"Anything for you, darlin'," he said and moved his finger against her. He felt her inner muscles clench around his cock then she screamed as she came and bit his neck, making him grunt. He came so hard, he was sure he blacked out for a few seconds. They both tried to catch their breaths as they sat there.

Scarlett lifted her head and looked into his eyes, and he knew he was falling in love with her. She lightly kissed his lips then smiled.

"That was hot," she said.

"It always is. Now my ass is probably dirty from sitting on this step," he said.

She burst out laughing. "Well, we can always take a shower, and I'll wash it for you."

He grinned. "As long as I get to return the favor."

"Deal." She slowly stood up and looked up to the door at the top. "I'm not sure I can climb these steps. You, Noah Conway, made me weak in the knees."

He got to his feet, pulled his jeans up, zipped them, picked her up, and tossed her over his shoulder.

"I'll get you there."

She laughed, making him grin.

"My hero," she said.

He smacked her on her ass as he climbed the steps.

"My clothes," she said.

"We'll get them tomorrow. It's not like anyone is going to see them. After a shower, we are going to sleep until noon."

"But my keys are in my jeans, and I need to unlock the door."

"Fuck," he muttered, set her on the step, turned, and headed back down to her clothes. He gathered them up and turned to walk back up the steps to where she sat but stopped when he saw her sitting there naked with her elbows on the step above her. "Shit."

"What's wrong, big boy? You don't like me sitting here waiting on you?" She slowly spread her legs and grinned at him.

"Hell, how is it possible to want you again so fast?"

She laughed low in her throat, and he was ready to take her on the steps again.

"You're making my damn dick hard again," he growled out.

"Why?" she asked him in an innocent tone, all the while opening and closing her legs.

He wasn't sure where he got the energy, but he ran up the steps, handed her the clothes, and helped her up.

"Just open the fucking door," he said.

Scarlett took her keys from the pocket of her jeans, opened the door, and laughed when he took her clothes from her, threw them on the floor, kicked the door closed, picked her up, and headed for the bedroom.

****

Later, as they lay in bed together, Scarlett had her head on his chest and sifted her fingers through the hair there. She couldn't stop thinking of how much this man meant to her. She knew she was falling for him, and it was the last thing he wanted. He didn't want to go through another heartache, even though she would never hurt him. She wished there was a

81

way to let him know that.

"What's going through that beautiful head of yours, Scarlett?"

His voice rumbled in her ear. She turned her head to look up at him.

"Nothing. Well, I was thinking about how hot the sex is with you."

"I'm surprised we don't set the place on fire," he said with a chuckle.

"You and me both."

"Hey, what was with the attitude toward Jeb tonight?"

Scarlett blew out a breath. "Nothing."

"Bullshit, Scarlett. I've never seen you act that way to someone you know. What is it?"

Sitting up, she adjusted the pillows against the headboard, leaned back against them, and pulled the blanket up to under her arms.

"You're going to think I'm nuts."

Noah scooted up against the headboard, took her hand in his, and kissed the palm.

"No, I won't. Tell me."

"I'm not certain, but I think Jeb is fucking around on Laura."

"Are you crazy?" he practically shouted.

"See? I don't know. That's why I didn't want to say anything. I could be imagining things. I just saw some things, and I have this gut feeling..." She shrugged.

"Just what things did you see?"

Scarlett told him about watching Jeb and Marie then she let out a sigh.

"I was sure I imagined things until they disappeared outside together and returned almost at the same time. I would never say

82

anything to Laura unless I caught him, but something is not right."

"You say he watches Marie?"

"Yes, and I know it's normal for men to look at a pretty woman, but the way he would smile at her..." She shook her head. "Then go outside at the same time. I'm going to continue to watch them. If I'm wrong, I'll be very happy about that, but if I'm right, I will personally cut his balls off."

Noah shook his head. "I find it hard to believe. He loves Laura."

"I keep telling myself that. I think the world of her, and I don't want to see her hurt, but I just noticed it so much lately."

"I'll watch too. I won't say anything to anyone either. For one, it's not my place, unless, but as you said, I catch him at it, then there will be hell to pay. I know how much Laura loves him."

"She even told me that she didn't want him there all the time she's working, but he said he was bored at home. Now I'm wondering if he just shows up so he can fuck Marie. Right under Laura's nose."

"Son of a bitch. Well, baby, I hope you're wrong."

"Not as much as I do. I forgot to tell you that Jayden Powers was in again."

"What? When?"

"The night we had the big snowstorm. He and his buddies came in. I was in the bar alone. It was right after I hung up from talking to you."

"He didn't do anything, did he? Because if he did, I will hunt him down and beat the hell out of him."

"No. He did ask where you were, and I told him

you were up here, waiting on me. I think he did plan on something, but they left when he thought you were here. Didn't even order a beer."

"I don't trust that little prick," Noah said through clenched teeth.

"I don't either. I panicked when they walked in, but I did tell him I was closing. They left, but Powers turned around and told me that he'd be back."

"Damn it. We'll keep an eye out for him." Noah slid back down, pulled her down with him, and kissed her lips.

"Let's get some sleep. I have an appointment tomorrow around one, or I should say later today."

"All right." She placed her head on his chest again and sighed when he wrapped his arms around her.

"I'll be going to Kalispell next week for a hunt. I'll be gone a week."

"Okay. I'll miss you," she whispered but knew he hadn't heard her because he'd fallen asleep.

****

When Noah returned from hunting, he got back to work on the saddle he had been working on. He had called Scarlett almost every day while he had been gone, and he was so ready to see her. He had missed her.

He arched his back and groaned when he heard bones crack. Damn, working on this saddle about did him in today. He walked to the sink, washed his hands, and dried them.

Noah smiled as he looked at the saddle. It had turned out great. The dark brown leather with pink stitching should make one little girl very happy. He had been working on it for months, and he needed to call the client so he could pick it up. His daughter's birthday was next week.

Walking around it, he made sure it was as it should be. Trick Dillon spoiled his daughter, Harlee, but he wanted it perfect, and Noah did his best. He removed his cellphone from his pocket and called him.

"Hey, Noah," Trick said when he answered.

"It's ready for you to look at, Trick."

"Great. Do you mind if I come over now? Harlee and Rayna are out shopping, so I'd like to do it while Harlee's gone. That way, I won't get a thousand questions on where I'm going and why she can't go with me."

Noah chuckled. "Sure. I'll be in the house." Noah removed the leather apron he wore when he worked on the tack.

"All right. I'll see you in a few minutes."

Noah disconnected then strode from the barn, across the yard, and up the steps. He wiped his feet on the mat, opened the door, and stepped into the warm kitchen. It was a bitterly cold day, but no snow was in the forecast for now. He knew that could change.

He made his way to his bedroom to change out of his dirty clothes. He got pretty messy when he worked on a saddle, even wearing the apron. After tossing the clothes into the hamper, he pulled on clean jeans and a T-shirt then headed for the kitchen to wait for Trick.

Hearing a vehicle pull up outside, Noah walked to the door, opened it, and saw Trick stepping from his truck. When he saw Noah in the doorway, he grinned.

"Hey, Noah."

"Trick. Would you like a cup of coffee?"

"Sure. The damn cold weather moved in quick." Trick trotted up the steps and wiped his feet on the mat.

Noah opened the door wider. "Hell yeah, it did. A man could freeze his balls off out there today, and I like mine too much to be out in it."

Trick chuckled. "I hear you."

"Take your coat off, Trick, and have a seat. It'll only take a minute."

"Thanks." Trick removed his hat and coat then hung them on a peg by the door. He pulled a chair out from the table and took a seat.

Noah made them both a cup of coffee. He placed a cup on the table in front of Trick, then he pulled a chair out and sat down. He watched Trick pick up the cup, blow on the hot brew then take a sip. Noah didn't know how Trick had survived going through his first wife's death a few years ago.

"Are you doing all right, Trick?"

Trick set the cup down and looked at him. "I am." He shook his head. "If someone would have told me that I'd fall in love and get married again, I think I would have punched them. I never thought I'd love someone as much as I loved Kaylee."

"I know you were devastated when she was killed in that accident."

"I didn't want to live, Noah, but I had to think of Harlee. The one thing I do regret is that Harlee will never know her mother. She does love Rayna, though."

"As you do."

86

"I do." Trick chuckled. "Fought it all the way too."

"I think we all do that."

"What about you, Noah? I heard you're seeing someone."

"No secrets in this town, is there?"

"Hell, no."

"I've been seeing Scarlett Robinson a while now. She bought Dewey's recently. He's her uncle."

"I haven't met her. I can't remember the last time I was in Dewey's." Trick cocked his head. "Is it serious?"

"I...like her."

"Like?"

"I can't do more, Trick."

"Bullshit."

"You know I've been through three damn engagements—"

"They weren't meant to be, Noah."

"And what if Scarlett isn't, either?"

"You won't know if you don't take a chance. Look, you know I loved Kaylee, but the thought of being alone the rest of my life didn't appeal to me but being with someone didn't either. I was between a rock and a hard place. I was so attracted to Rayna and pissed at myself for it. You're going to think I'm crazy, but Kaylee told me to be with Rayna."

"I don't think you're crazy, Trick. I believe Kaylee knew you needed to move on, even though you would always love her. Rayna is damn good for you."

"So, if I'm willing to take a chance, why aren't you?"

"Too chicken shit."

"Do you want another man to take her from you? Someone will snap her up. You can bet your ass on that. Take a chance, Noah."

Noah shoved the chair back, got to his feet, and stared down at his friend.

"I can't. The thought of going through another broken engagement scares the hell out of me, and it would hurt a lot more if it were with Scarlett."

Trick got to his feet. "That makes no fucking sense, Noah. You'll be without her anyway if you don't try."

"Let's go look at the saddle." Noah walked to where his coat hung on a peg.

"Conversation over, huh? All right. You're too damn hardheaded, Conway. Take it from another hardheaded man." Trick pulled on his coat, slapped his hat onto his head, and nodded for Noah to go.

Noah stared at him for a few seconds, opened the door, and they walked to the barn.

****

Another Saturday night, another packed crowd. Scarlett knew she shouldn't complain, but she didn't feel like she had time to breathe. Her uncle was helping tonight. She had called him to see if he would come in for a few hours since Laura was running late. She didn't tell Scarlett why and she didn't ask.

Scarlett hadn't talked to Noah in a few days, and she wondered what was going on with him. He was probably busy, but she had a feeling he was pulling back from her, and she knew he would eventually break it off with her.

"Hey, sorry I'm late," Laura said as she came behind the bar.

"It's fine. Are you all right?"

"Oh, yeah. I had some errands to run that I didn't get to earlier. If I had known we were this busy, I would have done them tomorrow."

"I didn't even see you come in," Scarlett said.

"How could you? I had trouble getting through the crowd."

"Well, I'm glad you're here now. Uncle Dewey can go home if he wants."

"I'll stick around a while," Dewey said as he passed them.

"I appreciate it." Scarlett smiled at him.

Laura touched her arm, making her look at her.

"Are *you* all right?"

"I haven't heard from Noah in a few days, and I have a feeling he's going to break it off with me. He's running scared. This is the first time he's done this. We've been seeing each other since late August, and it's November. He called me every day, even while he was on his hunting trip earlier this month, but it's been days. I called, left messages, and even sent him texts. He never answered."

"Oh, Scarlett, I hope he calls or comes in. You two are good together."

"I love him, Laura. I'd love to have him in my life. I want a family."

"You should tell him that. Maybe he would see the light if you did."

"I think I will. I mean, the worst he can do is leave me, and I've been preparing myself for that for quite a while."

"I'd tell him if I were you. He has to know where you stand."

"You're right. As soon as I see him, I'll tell him."

An hour later, she placed a beer down on the bar, took the cash from the man, turned to open the cash register, and saw Noah seated at the bar. After closing the drawer, she made her way to him.

"Hey, where have you been?"

"Busy," he said. "Can I get a beer?"

She frowned. "Of course."

Walking to the cooler, she slid it open, removed a frosted mug, poured a beer into it, and took it to him.

"Thanks." He picked it up and took a sip.

"I'd like to talk to you on my break if you don't mind."

He shrugged. "Sure."

Scarlett stared at him, but he turned on the stool to watch the crowd. If he thought he would be the one to break it off with her, he had better think again. Fifteen minutes later, she headed for him.

"Come to my office, please."

"Yes, ma'am." He got off the stool, strode around the bar, and followed her down the hall to her office.

Once inside, she closed the door, walked to her desk, pulled the chair out, and took a seat. Noah stood at the door.

"Have a seat," she said and pointed to the sofa.

"I'm fine right here. What did you want to talk about?"

"Well, I was wondering why I haven't heard

from you."

He shook his head and blew out a laugh.

"I told you, I was busy."

"And you couldn't just call or text me to let me know you were all right?"

"Christ, this sounds familiar," he muttered as he ran his hand around the back of his neck.

Scarlett got to her feet so fast that the chair spun around in circles behind her.

"Do not make me sound like them. I'm not complaining about you being busy, Noah. I was worried. I tried to call you, and I sent texts, but you ignored them," she snapped.

"What do you want me to say?"

"Nothing. Nothing at all. I've made up my mind that I'm done with this, Noah. I'm done waiting. We've been seeing each other for three months, and I can't do it anymore. I want to get married, and I want to have kids. Preferably with you, but I know that's not going to happen."

"Why am I not surprised? You said you were in no hurry to get married," he growled out.

"Well, I changed my fucking mind! You're a damn coward, Noah Conway. I'm going to find someone who wants what I do."

He reached for the doorknob behind him and opened the door. "Fine. You do that." He stepped out and slammed the door behind him.

Scarlett pulled the chair up behind her, collapsed onto it, and burst into tears.

A knock on the door startled her, but when it opened, Laura stuck her head in then entered and closed the door.

"Oh, what happened?"

"I told him what I wanted, and as you can see,

he took off like a bat out of hell. It's over, Laura."
She placed her hands over her face and cried.

"I'm so sorry. He's hardheaded. Maybe he'll come around." Laura put her arm around her.

"No, he won't. I called him a coward." She shook her head. "I shouldn't have said that."

"I wish I knew what to tell you, Scarlett. I'm so sorry. I can tell how much you love him. He's such a stubborn man."

Scarlett wiped the tears from her eyes and got to her feet.

"I suppose we had better get back out there."

They walked out of the office to behind the bar, but she didn't see Noah anywhere. He had not only walked out of her office and bar but also out of her life.

Chapter Five

As Noah drove home, he swore the entire way. After that talk with Trick, he knew he was getting in way over his head. He knew better. *Damn it.* He never stayed with one woman long. He didn't want them getting ideas, and Scarlett had.

"Son of a bitch," he muttered and hit his hand against the steering wheel.

She told him she would find someone who could give her what she wanted. Well, good for her.

"You're a fucking idiot, Conway."

As he pulled onto his driveway, he stopped the truck, leaned his head back, and wondered what the hell he would do without her in his life. He shouldn't have gone to bed with her more than once. Hell though, that first time was not enough, and he couldn't stay away. He didn't want her to find someone else. She was his, damn it.

Noah took a deep breath, drove up to the house, stepped out, and made his way inside. He took his hat off and then removed his coat and hung them on the pegs. He pulled a chair out with his foot, took a seat, rested his arms on his thighs, clasped his hands, and hung his head.

Sparky and Spike nudged his hands with their noses, and he looked at them.

"Hey, guys. I'm not good company right now. What am I supposed to do? I can't take the chance she'd break it off with me, just like the others did. I know, I know. I'm not with her now, but I wasn't given promises that weren't kept, at least this time. I'm better off alone."

He pushed to his feet, walked to his living room, took a seat in the recliner, and stared into the empty hearth. Shaking his head, he knew he would go into Dewey's again. He couldn't stay away. He had to make her see that she belonged to him, with or without a marriage proposal.

****

"Damn it," Scarlett swore as she spilled beer on the bar.

"You're not having a good night, hon," Dewey said with a wink.

"No, I'm not, Uncle Dewey. Too much on my mind."

Dewey moved to stand next to her and leaned close. "Scarlett, you've been out of sorts since you ended it with Noah. You were happy when you were with him."

"We don't want the same things. I need to move on."

"Uh, huh. I don't see that happening unless you move on with him."

"I can't do that. I have to find someone new."

Her uncle put his arm around her and squeezed. "I'm sure you can find someone, but you won't be happy. No matter what you tell yourself."

"I know. It's just what I have to do, though, Uncle Dewey."

"You'll need a man who doesn't mind that you own a bar," he said with a laugh.

"True. I have some weird hours."

Walking along the bar, she refilled drinks and

set bowls of peanuts and pretzels on the bar. She wished she could get Noah out of her mind. He was the most hardheaded man she'd ever met. Scarlett was nothing like those women who had broken his heart.

She had become good friends with his sister, Hailey, and she seemed to think they were gold diggers. Noah had money, but Scarlett couldn't care less. He could live paycheck to paycheck for all she cared. She loved *him*, not his damn money. Plain and simple.

Blowing out a frustrated breath, she decided to head for the back to get some liquor. It was getting low, and she didn't want to do it once the bar got more crowded. Tossing the bar rag down, she moved past her uncle and entered the back room. She didn't want her uncle trying to lift any of the boxes. They were heavy, but she was strong.

Squatting down, she picked up a box of Callahan Whiskey then headed back out to the bar. She almost dropped the box when she saw an old friend sitting there. She set it down and ran around the bar.

"Granger!" Scarlett yelled as she ran toward him and jumped into his arms.

Granger Crawford picked her up, spun her around, and set her on her feet.

"Damn, Scarlett, you get uglier every time I see you," he teased.

Laughing, Scarlett hugged him again. He had at one time held her heart. She met Granger when she was twenty-three, and he'd been twenty-nine. He wanted to marry her, but she wasn't ready for that. *If she knew then what she knew now.* She broke his heart, and she regretted that every day. He was a good man. He stood six-three, with dark blond hair and chocolate brown eyes.

"What are you doing here?"

"I was in the neighborhood," he said with a grin.

"Did you know I was here?"

"No. I just wanted to stop in and get a beer. It's a pleasant surprise, but not surprised to see you still bartending. How did you end up in Clifton?"

"My uncle used to own the bar. I bought it from him."

"You own the bar? That was something you always talked about."

"Yes, so when Uncle Dewey said he was going to retire, I offered to buy it. I like this little town. What are you doing here?" she repeated, took his hand, and led him to a barstool.

"I'm on my way to Kalispell to do some hunting."

"Kalispell?" She hoped he wasn't going with Noah.

"Yeah, I'm going on a guided hunt for elk and mule deer. You know I love to hunt. Well, if you remember that."

"I do remember. Who is your guide?" She held her breath.

"Buck, someone. Hell, I can't remember his last name, but it's with Conway Hunting."

"I know Noah Conway." *Boy, did she know him.*

"I never met the man. I just signed up online." Granger tilted his head. "Just how do you know him?"

"He's a...friend." The heat poured into her cheeks.

"Friend, huh? I'm thinking more than that. Did he hurt you, Scarlett?"

"Yes, but not intentionally. I fell in love. He didn't." She shrugged.

"I'm sorry. He must be an idiot not to fall for you."

Scarlett sighed. "No, he's not. It's not his fault he didn't fall in love with me. I wanted to marry him."

"Hell, I am sorry. I'm glad he's not my guide, then. I'd have to push him over a cliff."

Scarlett narrowed her eyes then grinned when she saw the humor in his eyes. "I hope you have a good time, though."

"I've wanted to go for years, but Sherry didn't like me going."

"Sherry?"

"My wife, well, ex-wife now. See, you should have married me."

"Maybe I should have."

He looked surprised but grinned. "Do you think we'd still be together?"

"Maybe."

"I loved you, Scarlett. I should never have let you go."

"I didn't give you a choice. When do you leave for your trip? I'd love to have dinner with you."

"I'd like that very much. I have a few days before I have to leave."

"I can meet you here. How about tomorrow night at six?"

"I'll be here," Granger said and pulled her into

another hug.

"I'll see you then." She kissed his cheek and watched him turn and walk out of the bar.

"Who was that?" Dewey asked her.

"Granger Crawford. I dated him years ago. He wanted to marry me."

"So why didn't he?"

"I wasn't ready. I was only twenty-three and in no hurry to settle down."

"Do you regret not marrying him?"

"No. I didn't love him enough to marry him, or I would have."

"Well, it seems like fate that he's come back into your life now when you do want to settle down."

Scarlett nodded but didn't say anything. Did it mean anything that Granger had come back into her life? Was he going to be her chance at happiness? She nibbled on her bottom lip as she thought of possibly trying to make it happen. He'd always been such a nice man and had a wonderful sense of humor. She had lost her virginity to him, and though he never failed to satisfy her, it hadn't been as mind-blowing as with Noah. Of course, she'd been so inexperienced that she didn't know what she was doing back then. Groaning, she put her hands over her face. No man was going to rock her world like Noah. After all, practice makes perfect. Most of her friends lost their virginity a lot sooner than she had, but her mother had been so strict and drilled it into her head that sex was wrong, and that's all men wanted.

After breaking up with Granger, she experimented with a few men, and something was still missing. That was until Noah Conway came into her life. That man could burn her up with a look. He knew what to do with a woman, and she knew she'd never have that with another man. She remembered having a talk with Hailey about sex. How it should be and how the man shouldn't just be in it for himself. Hailey was happily married to Gage Beckett, and she'd told Scarlett that she knew what Scarlett meant because sex with Gage was amazing. Chemistry meant a lot. Hailey never had it with her ex-fiancé, Tony, but she did with Gage. Scarlett was so happy for her friend, but she wanted that too. With Hailey's big brother, Noah.

On Sunday evening, Granger picked her up at the bar. Even though a door outside led up to her apartment, she would rather have him meet her here. She opened the door to let him in, and when he entered, he handed her a bouquet of daisies.

"You remembered I love daisies," she said.

"I remember everything about you, Scarlett."

Scarlett stared up at him and watched him lower his head. Then he pressed his lips to hers. She wrapped her arms around his neck, but it just didn't thrill her as Noah's kisses. She pulled back from him.

"That was nice," she said.

"I thought so. Let's eat. I got us into a restaurant in a town called Hartland. They had a cancellation, so I was lucky to call when I did."

"I know the Hartland Restaurant well. It has great food."

"Good. If you're ready, we can go."

"Let me put these in water first and get my

coat."

"It's cold out there." Granger stood by the door while she put the flowers, along with water, in a beer mug then grabbed her coat.

She shrugged it on and tightened her lips as she thought about Noah always holding her coat for her. Mentally shaking her head, she knew she had to stop thinking about that man. She smiled up at Granger.

"I'm ready when you are."

"Let's go then. I'm hungry."

As they sat in the restaurant, she looked over the menu and barely concentrated on it. She missed Noah so much, but she had to move on. He was never going to marry her.

"You're a million miles away, Scarlett."

"I'm sorry. Just wondering what to get."

"You're going to go with that, huh?"

She placed the menu on the table and looked at him.

"I'm sorry. My mind is on...other things."

"Conway?"

"Yes. You know, Granger, I'm sorry I hurt you because now I know how you felt."

"It was a long time ago, Scarlett."

"I want to get married. I want to have kids, but that won't happen with Noah."

"It could happen with me," Granger said quietly.

"What?"

"Just hear me out. I'm not going to lie to you. I'm still in love with my wife, but I know I have to move on, just like you do." He shrugged. "Why not with each other? I'll give you marriage and kids. I'm sure it wouldn't take much for me to fall in love with you again."

"I don't know…"

"You have a better choice? No offense, hon, but you're not getting any younger, and neither am I. I'd like to have kids before I'm too old to enjoy them. We know each other. Hell, we have always gotten along great, and I wouldn't mind having you in my life again."

"Why didn't you have kids while you were married?"

"Sherry was too into her career."

"But I'm busy too, Granger. I have my bar."

"But you also want kids. Right?"

"I do."

Should she do it? Marry a man she didn't love? But the man she loved didn't want to marry her. She'd never be Mrs. Noah Conway or have his children, and that about killed her, but it was a fact. She stared at Granger. She had loved him at one time. Could she again?

"We haven't seen each other in years, Granger."

"So? We know each other. It's not like I'm a stranger asking you to marry me. If you tell me no, I'll walk out of your life, and you'll never hear from me again, but you know Conway isn't going to marry you. I will."

"What happens if Sherry says she wants you back?"

Granger blew out a laugh. "That's not going to happen. Trust me, I tried."

"Okay." Scarlett stared at him. "Can I think about it?"

"Of course, you can. You can let me know tomorrow." He winked at her.

She laughed. "Maybe I will." She tilted her head. "What happened to your marriage? If you don't mind my asking."

Granger blew out a breath. "I'm not sure. I was crazy about Sherry. One day I came home from work, and she told me she wanted a divorce. You could have knocked me over with a feather. I asked her why and the only thing she would say was, we drifted apart. I don't know. I was working a lot at the time. Maybe she got lonely." He shrugged.

Scarlett thought about the women Noah had been engaged to, telling him the same thing. Didn't some women realize that their man was trying to provide for them?

"She never said more than that?"

"No. I didn't contest the divorce, so it was over faster than the wedding, it seemed. I loved her."

"It sounds like you didn't want the divorce."

"I didn't, but I didn't want to hold her back if she wanted to move on."

"Did she?"

"As far as I know, she's still single and not seeing anyone." He shook his head. "I don't know what brought it on."

"Maybe you two will talk about it again one day."

"I don't think so. She moved to Billings, so I never see her or hear from her."

Once they ordered their food, they talked about old times. Granger could always make her laugh. Would it be such a hardship being married to him?

****

If Noah had gone hunting, maybe his mind

wouldn't be on Scarlett so much. Damn, he missed that woman. He hadn't slept worth a shit for the past two weeks. He wanted to go into town to see her, but he knew it was a waste of time because he couldn't give her what she wanted. If he could, he'd do it in a heartbeat, but he was scared shitless about trying again. Love didn't last. At least, not for him. Women just loved to break his heart, and he had a feeling if Scarlett broke it, it would never mend.

"Hey, boss."

Noah turned to see his ranch manager in the doorway.

"What's up, Brad?"

"I just wanted to let you know the hay is stacked, and we checked the fence. All's good."

"Great. One less thing for me to worry about." Noah strolled to him, and Brad moved aside.

"I'm heading home if that's all right."

"Of course, it is. I'm heading in myself."

"The boys are heading to Dewey's. Do you want to go?" Brad grinned.

"No. I'm staying in tonight." Noah started walking down the aisle, and Brad walked beside him.

"You do know that Scarlett is seeing someone else now, right?"

Noah stopped in his tracks.

"What? Who?"

"His name is Granger Crawford. She introduced me to him a few nights ago."

"I don't know him," Noah said as pain ripped through his chest.

"I can't believe you're letting that woman go. You had a good thing with her. You're just too

103

fucking hardheaded to admit it." Brad turned away and strode down through the barn.

Noah sighed. Brad didn't understand. No one did. He couldn't risk another broken heart, especially from Scarlett. It was best if he stayed the hell away from her, which made no sense because he was hurting now without her. But he hated hearing she was seeing someone else.

Blowing out a frustrated breath, he strolled from the barn to head for his house. When he stepped into the sunshine, the cold slammed into him. He tugged his collar up on his sheepskin jacket, pulled his hat lower, and then picked up his pace to get to the house.

He jogged up the steps, wiped his feet on the mat, opened the door, and entered the kitchen, sighing at the warmth. Sparky and Spike sat staring up at him. Grinning, he took his hat and coat off and hung them up. Then he pulled a chair out from the kitchen table, took a seat, and toed off his boots. Picking them up, he pushed to his feet and carried the boots into the mudroom. He set them inside the door, then reentered the kitchen and stared at the dogs.

"I suppose you think you deserve biscuits," Noah said, laughing. The dogs knew not to do anything until he said anything. They patiently sat on the rug, waiting for their master to pet them. Noah reached down and rubbed both their ears, then they stood and spun in circles. He turned and reached into the box sitting by the door and handed them each a biscuit. After giving them the treats, he headed for the bathroom to take a hot shower.

He strode down the hallway to his bedroom

and entered the bathroom, where he stripped off his clothes. Reaching into the shower stall, he turned the water on, and steam filled the room. Pulling the door open, he stepped inside and moaned as the hot water hit between his shoulder blades. Then he turned the knob to have the other showerhead spray on him too. He picked up the shampoo, squirted some in his hand then scrubbed his hair. After rinsing it, he reached for the soap and scrubbed his tired body clean. He shut the water off, opened the door, took a navy blue towel from the rack, ran it over his head, then down his body. He wrapped it around his waist and made his way to the mirror over the sink. Swiping his hand across it to see, he picked up his razor and stared at himself in the mirror.

Scarlett always seemed to be on his mind. Damn it. He couldn't shake her from his mind. Did she miss him at all? Well, not if she was seeing someone new. He refused to admit to his feelings for her, convinced if he kept them in, his heart wouldn't be broken.

"What a load of shit that is," he said to his reflection. There would never be another woman for him. Scarlett was it. Even if she did find someone else, she'd always have Noah's heart. "Fuck this. I'll let it grow," he muttered as he tossed the razor onto the counter.

A few days later, Noah walked out of the barn and swore when he saw snow falling. It was accumulating fast. Striding across the yard, he climbed the steps, stomped the snow from his boots, opened the door, and entered the warm kitchen. The dogs didn't get up from the floor as he took his hat and coat off then hung them up on the pegs.

"Well, you two sure know how to make a guy feel welcome," he said and grinned when both their tails thumped on the floor, but they didn't even raise their heads.

He pulled a chair out from the table with his foot, plopped down on it toed, his boots off, and removed his socks. Pushing to his feet, he unsnapped his jeans, lowered the zipper, and removed them. He strode to the mudroom, tossed them in the hamper, then removed his flannel shirt and the T-shirt underneath. After throwing everything into the hamper, he walked barefoot through the kitchen, living room, and down the hall to head for his bathroom. He needed a hot shower and then food. It had been one hell of a long day, and he hadn't stopped for lunch. His stomach growled. Breakfast had been a long time ago.

After his shower, he pulled on clean sweatpants and a T-shirt then headed for the kitchen to get something to eat. He yanked on the fridge door and looked inside, but all he saw was stuff to make sandwiches. Sighing, he picked up the meat, cheese, and mustard and placed them on the counter.

Once his sandwich was ready, he opened the fridge again, removed a beer, opened it, picked up his sandwich, and headed for the living room. He took a seat in the recliner, lifted the footrest, aimed the remote at the TV, and bit into his sandwich.

Damn it. He missed that woman, and he would love to give her anything she wanted.

There was just one thing he couldn't.

"What the fuck is wrong with you?" he muttered.

He knew there would never be another woman like Scarlett in his life. But after what the other three did to him, he was too afraid to take another chance, especially with Scarlett. If he asked her to marry him and she said yes, and broke his heart, he'd be a broken man, and that wasn't a chance he was willing to take.

"Do you want her to be with another man?" Noah shook his head. "Hell, no."

He'd been talking to himself a lot more lately. Ever since she'd told him that it was over, she was done waiting for him to grow some balls and take another chance. He couldn't blame her. She had been waiting months, and he still couldn't get his ass in gear.

"Son of a bitch," he swore. "You're going to lose her for good if you don't do something, and soon."

He wasn't sure what his problem was as far as Scarlett was concerned. He didn't want another man to take his woman, and she *was* his woman, damn it. He was too scared to get engaged again. Every time he thought he'd found the right woman, his heart was ripped out. It was the same shit with each of them. He spent too much time in the barn. He was away hunting too much. He never paid attention to them. Damn, you'd think he'd learn not to go through it a third fucking time, but he always thought it would be different with the next one, and it never was. That was why he wouldn't do it again. Because of how he felt about Scarlett, he couldn't chance it. If she left him, he'd want to curl into a ball and die.

"Yet, you're without her now, genius," he muttered.

When his cellphone buzzed, he looked at it to see his sister's face. Smiling, he hit *Answer.*

"Hey, kiddo. How's married life?"

"Wonderful. You should try it sometime."

"Yeah, right."

"How are you doing?"

"I'm good. What's up? Is Beckett good to you?"

Hailey laughed. "Of course, he is."

"He'd better, or I'll kick his ass."

"Yeah, I believe that's why he is."

Noah chuckled. "He's a smart man."

"Don't forget Mom and Dad's wedding anniversary next month. We're all going to the Hartland Restaurant. You'll be there, right?" she asked him.

Noah ran his hand around the back of his neck.

"Sure, I'd love to. Just let me know when."

"I'll call you. I love you, big brother."

"I love you too, sis. See you then."

"Wait. Why don't you see Scarlett anymore?"

"Shit, Hailey, mind your own business," he snapped.

"Excuse me? You practically threatened Gage when you found out we were seeing each other. Scarlett and I have become good friends, and she is hurting."

"Me threatening Gage is not the same—"

"Bullshit, Noah. You're my brother, Scarlett is my friend, so it is my business," Hailey practically shouted.

"If you're such good friends with her, then you know she broke it off, not me."

"Because you won't marry her. Noah, you are an idiot letting her go. I had never seen you so happy. You need to get your ass in gear and get her back before she marries Granger."

Noah sat up so fast that the footrest on the recliner slammed shut.

"Marry him?"

"She told me he asked her."

"Doesn't mean she will."

"What other option does she have? You haven't put a ring on her finger. I think you need to talk to her. I'll call you about the dinner." She disconnected.

He hit *End* and put the phone on the arm of the chair.

"Son of a bitch," he roared.

Blowing out a breath, he pushed himself up from the chair and decided to hit the sheets. It was just too bad a certain gray-eyed redhead wasn't hitting them with him. He was definitely horny.

"Damn it, Scarlett."

Striding down the hall, he entered his bedroom to see Spike and Sparky already on the floor in front of the fireplace. They looked up with goofy dog grins on their faces then put their heads on their paws. Noah made his way to the bed, sat on the edge, clasped his hands, and rested his arms on his thighs. God, he loved her. He just couldn't ask her to marry him. He wished it were different.

"It is what it is," he whispered.

Damn, he hurt. He missed her so much, but

he knew if he asked her to marry him, they'd never make it to the altar. She'd find an excuse to leave him too. They always do. Why couldn't she just let it be? Why ruin a good thing?

He would go to the bar one night and talk her into coming back to him. Falling back on the bed, he stared up at the ceiling. With a smile, he sat up, stood, and removed his clothes, crawled between the sheets, and waited for sleep to overtake him.

****

Scarlett served a cowboy a beer, turned to put the money in the cash register when she saw Noah taking a seat at the bar, and she almost dropped the money. God, he looked so good. It had been too long since she'd seen him. Over two months, to be exact. She took a deep breath and made her way to him.

"Hey, cowboy. What can I get you?"

He looked into her eyes, and her heart hit her stomach. She missed him so much.

"A bottle of beer, Scarlett," he said in a low tone of voice, and she had to suppress a shiver. She used to love hearing him whisper in her ear.

"Uh, okay. I'll be right back." She walked to where Laura stood and stopped beside her. "Will you get Noah a beer from the cooler? I need a break."

"Sure," Laura said with a frown.

Scarlett quickly made her way back to her office, opened the door, entered, and closed it behind her. She leaned back against it as tears rolled down her cheeks. Why was he here? She wanted to hide away so she didn't have to look at his handsome face and know she'd never have him in her life again.

With a sob, she pushed off the door, walked to her desk, pulled the chair out, and plopped down on it. A knock on the door startled her, and she quickly wiped the tears away.

"Who is it?" she called out, afraid it would be Noah.

"Laura."

"Come in"

The door opened, and Laura entered.

"What's going on?"

"I can't look at him, Laura. I just can't." She shook her head.

Laura strode to the couch and took a seat.

"Scarlett, you need to tell him about you and Granger."

"I'm not sure I can."

"You have to. Noah is here for one reason. *You.* He needs to know that you're going to marry another man." Laura tilted her head. "Unless you're not."

"I'm going to marry Granger. I want a family, Laura. I want stability. Noah can't give me either."

After a week of some heavy thinking, she had decided to marry Granger. She was going to take that chance.

"Then you owe it to Noah to tell him."

"You're right. I know you're right. It's just that it's going to be so hard to look into that face and tell the man I love that I'm going to marry someone else."

"I don't envy you, that's for sure." Laura got to her feet. "I'd better get back out there."

"I'll be out in a minute."

"All right." Laura opened the door, stepped out, and closed it behind her.

Scarlett sat there for a few more minutes, pushed the chair back, stood, and walked to the door. She reached for the doorknob, opened the door, stepped into the hall then came to a stop when she saw Noah leaning against the opposite wall with his arms folded across his broad chest.

"What are you doing back here?" she asked.

"Looking for you, why else?"

"I need to get back to the bar." She started past him, but he wrapped his fingers around her wrist. She refused to look up at him. She loved this man, but he didn't love her. She knew she had to move on as much as that killed her.

"I heard you were seeing someone. Who the hell is Granger Crawford?" Noah asked her.

"I was involved with him years ago, and just how do you know about him?"

"And he just happened to come back into your life," Noah practically growled.

"How do you know about him?" she repeated.

"Hell, this is Clifton. Not much gets by people in this town or the other two.

"He wants to marry me," she whispered.

"And?"

"And I'm going to marry him."

"Is that right?"

"You know he's not my first choice, but my first choice doesn't want to marry me."

"Damn it, Scarlett. You know how I feel about it."

"I know," she said, and her voice caught.

"I don't want you to marry him. I don't want to lose you."

112

She looked up at his handsome face and could see the pain etched there. A tear slid down her cheek.

"I just can't do this, Noah. I told you, I need stability in my life, and I don't have that with you. I'm sorry." She started to move away, but he wrapped his hand around her bicep to stop her.

****

Noah turned her so that her back was against the wall, and he placed his hands on the wall on each side of her head, leaned in close to her, and stared into her eyes.

"So tell me, Scarlett," he moved his lips close to her ear. "Does he make you scream in bed like I do? Does he make you want that orgasm so bad that you bite him like you do me?" He grinned when she shivered. "Does he make you beg?"

"Noah, stop—"

"Because if he doesn't, sweetheart, you'd better remember that's how boring your sex life will be if you marry him. You need a man in your bed who's as wild as you are, and you and I both know that's me."

Scarlett's hands pressed against his shoulders and pushed, making him step back.

"Then *you* marry me, Noah. If you're so worried about what my sex life will be like without you, then you marry me," she said and shoved him harder and walked away from him.

He watched her walk back out to the bar.

"Son of a bitch," he muttered as he put his back against the wall and hung his head.

Taking a deep breath, he straightened up and strode out of the hall to the bar. He resumed his seat and watched her as she moved around behind the bar, filling orders. She never looked his way, and he wondered if he'd pushed her too hard. But damn it, he didn't want her marrying another man. She belonged to him.

"Could I get a beer?" he called out. He watched her take a deep breath, but she moved further down the bar away from him. Fuck, she was hardheaded.

"Here ya go, Noah," Keith said as he set a beer down in front of him.

"Thanks, Keith." Noah twisted the bottle around in his hand and kept his eyes on Scarlett. Clenching his jaw when she laughed at something some cowboy said to her, he knew he didn't feel like kicking someone's ass tonight, but if that cowboy didn't back off, there was going to be hell to pay. Pushing to his feet, he narrowed his eyes and stared at them. He was just about to make a move to where they stood when Scarlett stepped away from him and moved to the cash register.

An hour later, he still sat at the bar with the same beer Keith had given him and watched as Scarlett worked. Not once did she look at him. He slammed the bottle onto the bar making the froth spill over the top and flow down over the bottle and onto the bar. People at the bar glanced over to him, but when he glared at them, they all looked away. Keith came to him and wiped the bar off.

"Sorry, Keith," he muttered.

"No worries, Noah," Keith said with a smile.

Noah reached into his back pocket for his wallet, pulled out a twenty, and laid it on the bar.

"Keep the change," he said, turned from the

114

bar, shoved through the crowd, pushed the door open, and headed outside.

Chapter Six

Noah looked at the clipboard then at the eight men standing before him. Their duffle bags sat on the ground beside them. He wanted to be anywhere but here. Damn Scarlett for telling him she was going to marry another man.

"Two men per cabin."

"Does it matter who we bunk with?" one man asked.

Noah mentally shook his head. *Why would it matter?*

"No. I know a few of you came together, so sort it out. I'll be in the first one," Noah said as he pointed to the cabin that sat a little way from the others.

"You don't bunk with anyone?" another man asked.

"No. I put up with you all day. I'm not staying in the same cabin with you at night." He grinned, and the men laughed.

He glanced down at the list again and clenched his jaw when he saw the name. He raised his head and glanced at each man.

"Which one of you is Granger Crawford?"

"I am," the man said, stepping forward.

Noah wanted to punch him. This man thought he was going to take Scarlett from him. He gave him a nod.

"All right. Pick your cabins," Noah snapped and watched as the men frowned at him, then picked up their bags and headed for the cabins.

"Can I ask why you wanted to know which one I was?" Crawford asked him.

Noah stared at him. Though not quite as tall, Crawford stood a little over six feet, with dark blond hair and brown eyes. He didn't seem like Scarlett's type.

"I know Scarlett," he said with a shrug and wanted to wrap his hand around the man's throat when he grinned.

"You wouldn't happen to be Noah Conway, would you?"

"I am."

"What happened to the man who was supposed to guide us?"

"Buck had a family emergency, not that it's any of your business."

Crawford stepped forward, and Noah had to give him credit. The man had balls.

"I'm going to marry her."

"Good luck with that," Noah snarled.

"Well, it doesn't look like you're going to, Mr. Conway."

"Maybe not, but I'd lay money on *you* not marrying her, *Mr.* Crawford." He turned from him then turned back. "Please get settled in. We leave at dawn."

"Yes, sir. I'll be ready...for anything."

Noah watched him walk off and enter a cabin. *Son of a bitch.* He hoped Crawford went home empty-handed.

The next morning, the men met in the larger cabin for breakfast. Noah shook his head at the ones yawning. *This ought to be good.* Then he saw Crawford, and he looked ready to go. Noah clenched his jaw and took a seat with four other

117

men.

"Your rifles are out front," Noah told them.

"So, where are we going?" one of them asked.

"Up through the north passage. There are some big elk and mule deer up there." Noah stabbed his fork into his scrambled eggs.

"Just how do we get an animal back if we're going on horseback?" Crawford asked him.

"We radio back here, and the men will come and get it in a truck. *If* you get one."

"Wouldn't it be easier if we just took a truck up there?"

Noah clenched his jaw. "Where we're going, you can't get to it in a truck—"

Crawford laughed. "Then how are the men here going to get it?"

Noah shot to his feet. "They will get as close as they can, then hike in and drag the animal out. Did you read the brochure, Crawford?"

The place went silent as Noah stared at him.

"I guess I missed that part. It just seems like it's unnecessary," Crawford said with a shrug.

"You can always leave, but you do forfeit your payment." Noah resumed his seat and picked up his fork.

"Oh, no, Mr. Conway. You are not getting rid of me that easily."

Noah looked over to him, but he had his head down, and Noah was sure he was hiding a grin. He knew damn well Noah knew he wasn't talking about the hunting expedition. *Son of a bitch!*

He can't remember ever wanting to hit someone this bad. Noah wasn't a violent man, he usually tried to walk away, but this guy aggravated the hell out of him. Crawford was egging him on, and he was letting him.

Taking a deep breath, he blew it out and continued to eat his breakfast even though he had no appetite, but he knew they all needed to get some food in them. It was damn cold, and it would be colder the higher they rode.

Once everyone finished eating, they met outside, where the men who worked for Noah had the horses ready. They handed each man a thick scarf for their faces.

"Pick your horse," he told the hunters.

"I'd like that black one," Crawford said.

"He's mine. Pick another one," Noah all but growled out.

"Sure. You just said pick a horse, so I did."

Noah spun around to look at him, walked to where he stood, and stopped within feet of him.

"Do not push me, Crawford."

"Is that what I'm doing?" Crawford's eyebrows shot up.

"Just get on a fucking horse," Noah said through clenched teeth and fisted his gloved hands when Crawford chuckled and walked to a horse.

Noah strode to his horse, vaulted into the saddle, and watched as the men mounted up and the workers handed each man a rifle and showed them how to put it in the sheath alongside the saddle.

As much as he hated to admit it, Crawford sat a horse well. The other men were another matter altogether. Three looked terrified, and four looked like they would throw up. He never understood the people who came on these trips and had never been on a horse. The brochure

119

clearly stated that horseback riding was how they made their way to the elk and mule deer. Luckily, all the horses were gentle. He kneed his horse over to one of the men.

"Relax. You'll be sore as hell if you don't. The horse is gentle. All you have to do is sit there, and she'll follow behind the others," Noah told the man.

"All right. Never been on a horse in my life."

"You'll be a pro at it by the end of the week." Noah looked at the other men. "Just give the horse a little nudge with both knees, and they'll follow my horse. Let's get going."

He nudged his horse then turned in the saddle to see the others following. He noticed Crawford at the back of the line, and he grinned when he saw Noah looking at him. Noah turned around and huffed out a breath. He pulled the thick scarf up around his nose. Maybe Crawford would freeze to death out here.

Later as they headed back, the men were all talking to Crawford on the elk he had bagged. Of all the men on the trip, Crawford was the only one to get an animal. Damn it. Any other time, Noah would be happy to see one of the hunters get an elk but not this time.

They rode back to camp, dismounted, and headed for their cabins. Noah helped his workers unsaddle the horses.

"Conway."

Noah huffed and turned to look at Crawford. "What is it?"

"I appreciate you dressing the elk for me."

"I do it for anyone getting an animal. You're not special."

120

Crawford chuckled. "You don't like me, do you?"

"Is it that obvious?" Noah snapped.

"You know, if you're so upset that she's going to marry another man, maybe you should do something about that."

"Maybe you should mind your own fucking business," Noah said through clenched teeth.

"Where Scarlett is concerned, it is my business." Crawford turned away from him then back. "She loves *you*. You big dumbass, but I'll take my chances that she'll eventually get over you and love me again."

Noah watched him walk off then enter the cabin. *Fuck! What man marries a woman who loves someone else? What man lets a woman marry another man when he loves her?* He snorted.

"Dumbass is right," he muttered as he led his horse to the small stable.

Later in the week, two of the other men bagged mule deer, and another got an elk. Noah grinned as they took pictures using their phones.

"There's no feeling quite like getting one of those."

Noah glanced to his right to see Crawford sitting on his horse next to him.

"No, there isn't," Noah said.

"How many have you gotten?"

Noah blew out a laugh. "A few."

"Bulls?"

"Yes, and a few cows." He glanced over to Crawford and back to the other men. "I have a monarch above my mantle," he said with pride.

"Holy hell! A sixteen-point? Damn."

121

"Probably the only one I'll ever get with that many. Hell, I didn't even know it was a sixteen point until I got to him after I shot."

"I'd love to get one of those or an imperial."

"Fourteen points is nice too, but you did get a twelve-point, so you got a royal."

"Yeah, but we always want what we don't have, don't we?"

"I suppose," Noah murmured.

"You know, you should marry that woman before you lose her to me," Crawford said with a smirk.

Before Noah could reply, Crawford rode his horse closer to the men, dismounted, walked to them, and shook their hands.

"Mind your own damn business," Noah muttered as he dismounted, radioed in for the men to bring the trucks, then walked to where the hunters stood and began dressing the animals.

****

Scarlett stood at the bar, watching the crowd. Her mind was on Noah and Granger. She wondered how the trip went. Granger had sent her a text telling her that Noah was leading the hunting group.

"Hey, are you all right?" Laura asked her.

"Yeah, I'm just thinking."

"About what? Or should I say who?"

Scarlett looked at her. "I'm wondering how the hunting trip went. Granger sent me a text to tell me that Noah was filling in for one of the other guides, and he didn't seem happy with Granger at all."

"Oh, they know each other by name, don't

they?"

"Yes. Noah knew Granger's name, and of course, Granger knows all about Noah." She shook her head. "I hope they didn't get into it."

"Well, you can find out. Noah just came in." Laura jerked her chin toward the door.

Scarlett looked over to see Noah heading for the bar. Then he took a seat on one of the stools.

"Do you want me to wait on him?" Laura asked her.

"No. I'll do it."

She took a deep breath, walked to where he sat, and stopped in front of him.

"What would you like, Noah?"

"Beer."

"On tap?"

"Yeah."

She frowned at him then turned away to get his beer. She kept stealing glances at him, but he wasn't even looking at her. He had spun around on the stool to watch the crowd. If he didn't want to talk to her, why come in here? She walked to him, set the frosty mug on the bar, and stared at him. He didn't even turn around on the stool.

"How was your hunting trip? Did you get anything?"

Noah spun around on the stool to face her.

"No, but your...*fiancé* did," he said and picked up the mug.

She didn't miss that he had stressed fiancé. Well, two could play this game.

"I didn't know that. I'll have to congratulate him when I see him later."

Noah's head snapped up, and his eyes

123

narrowed.

"Yeah, you do that." He turned around to watch the dance floor again. The next time she looked to where he had sat, he was gone.

The next weekend, Scarlett scanned the bar and shook her head. It never failed to pack people in. No matter what the weather. It was snowing, yet these people were, drinking, dancing, and having a good time.

She opened the cash register, then glanced along the bar and saw Noah raising his hand to her. She slammed the drawer closed, took a deep breath, and walked to where he sat.

"What can I get you, Noah?"

He stared at her so long that she started to fidget.

"I shouldn't have to tell you that, Scarlett," he said in a low tone of voice.

"I'll get you a beer," she said and started to turn away when he wrapped his fingers around her wrist, making her look at him. She raised an eyebrow.

"You and I both know I'm not talking about a damn beer."

Scarlett leaned close to him. "I do know, but I also know this is over. I told you that I can't do it anymore."

"You agreed, Scarlett." Noah stared at her. "You knew how I felt about it."

"Yes, and I honestly thought I could do it. I wanted you, Noah, but I want more. You're not prepared to give me that."

"You knew," he practically growled.

"So you think you can just come in here and go upstairs with me. Is that it?" She jerked her wrist from his hand. "I will not be a piece of ass for you whenever you get the urge. I got in too deep, and you broke my heart."

Noah shook his head. "Like you didn't break mine."

"No woman can break your heart. You're a hard man."

"Seriously? It's been broken three fucking times. Four if I count you."

"It's not my fault that it's broken now," she snapped.

"You know it's damn good between us."

"Between the sheets, you mean."

He shrugged. "You can't deny it."

"It was the best I ever had," she whispered.

"Then why not again?"

"My biological clock is ticking. I want kids. I bought this bar from my uncle so I'd have some stability in my life, but I want more. You are not willing to give me that."

"It's like beating a dead horse with you."

Scarlett stared at that handsome face. "One day, a woman is going to make you beg, Noah Conway. I just hope I'm around to see it."

"Oh, come on, Scarlett. You've made me beg." His eyes met hers.

"Not the way I'm talking about, but it was fun having my way with you." She shrugged. "I want...*need* more." She reached her hand out and touched his bearded cheek. "You need to shave this off. I don't like it."

"So if I shave it, can I stay tonight?"

"No."

"Then why should I shave it?"

"You shouldn't hide that gorgeous face." She

shrugged. "Maybe some other woman would like it, but I don't. I've never been into thick beards."

"It's not even that thick."

"I like some sexy stubble, but even this..." she touched his cheek again. "Is too thick for me. My skin would get irritated."

"Well, since I love going all over that sexy body of yours, I'll shave just for you."

"You do that, but this is not happening." She waved her hand between them.

"Shit. I'm leaving. I can't sit here and talk with you about sex and know we won't be having any." He pushed to his feet, pulled his wallet from his back pocket, and paid for his beer. She watched him push his way through the crowd to the doors, then they opened, and he disappeared.

Looking back, Scarlett knew she should never have gotten involved with him, but once he had her in bed, she couldn't resist him. As she told him, it was the best sex she ever had, and any time he came around, she'd go home with him or take him upstairs.

She hadn't lied when she told him he'd broken her heart. He just didn't know to what extent. She loved him, and she had a feeling no other man would compare to him in any way. He told her from the beginning that he never wanted to get married. He'd been hurt too many times, and he never had luck in love. He had been honest from the start, and she thought she could handle it until she couldn't and decided to break it off. She couldn't take it anymore and told him she needed more. She knew she would never be able to convince him that she would never hurt him.

Scarlett wished he would stay out of the bar. She hated seeing him and not being with him. No man would ever have her heart. Even though she would marry Granger, Noah owned her heart.

****

Noah made his way to his truck, hit the fob to unlock it then climbed in. He wrapped his hands around the steering wheel and squeezed them until they hurt. Damn it! The one thing he didn't want to do, he had. He had fallen in love with her, but the thought of her leaving him just tore him apart.

"Like she's in your life now, jackass," he muttered as he started the truck and drove home.

The following Saturday, Noah told himself there was no way he was going to Dewey's. All he was asking for was trouble. He knew Scarlett would not hop into bed with him. He missed her so much. They had fantastic chemistry, but she wanted more, and she would have it with Crawford.

"She knew, damn it. I made it clear from the beginning," he murmured.

"Hey, boss."

Noah turned to see Brad standing in the doorway.

"What's up, Brad?"

"I just wanted to let you know that the men took the horses to the east pasture. Since the snow has tapered off, and it's supposed to quit later."

"That's fine. I'm going to finish this saddle and take the rest of the day off."

"You? Taking a day off?" Brad grinned when

Noah narrowed his eyes.

"Yes, smartass. I don't have anymore I can work on right now."

"You still have orders, though, right?"

"Oh, yeah, but the leather isn't ready yet."

"Okay. I'm heading for the other barn to muck out the stalls. Call me if you need me."

"Will do."

Noah watched Brad leave as he picked up a rag to wipe his hands off. He turned to stare at the saddle but didn't see it. His mind was on Scarlett, as usual. She had agreed to not expect more from him, then suddenly, she wants more, and since he won't give it to her, she's going to marry Crawford. Damn her for wanting more. He was sure she would be in his life a lot longer.

Maybe he just needed to accept it. She was going to marry another man, and there was nothing Noah could do about it. She had to know how he felt about her. He just didn't want to take that step to marriage. Hell, it wasn't the marriage part. It was the engagement. He knew, without a doubt, that if he put a ring on her finger, she'd end up breaking the engagement. It was inevitable.

God, he loved her, though, and she had to know that. Just because he didn't want to put a ring on her finger didn't mean he didn't love her. How could she not know? She was the only woman he saw. Wasn't that commitment? Hell, who knows how a woman thinks? No man did, that was for sure. He quit trying to figure them out years ago. It was best to sit back and let them do their thing. He huffed out a sigh. Scarlett would always have his heart.

****

Scarlett set a drink down in front of a woman then turned to wait on someone else. Laura was hustling behind the bar too. Scarlett hadn't seen Jeb yet tonight, and she wondered why. She moved to the cooler to get a beer out. Laura reached in before Scarlett slid the lid closed.

"God, it is so busy tonight." Laura laughed.

"Yes, it is. Where's Jeb?"

Laura straightened up and looked at her. "He said he wasn't coming in tonight."

"Seriously? Why?"

"He said he knew I didn't want him here every time I was here. I was shocked. I'm glad, though. I don't need him watching my every move. I love him, but damn, sometimes I need a break."

"Yes, you do."

"I'd better get this beer to that cowboy; he keeps staring at me." Laura smiled.

"Yeah, I need to serve this too."

Scarlett was a little shocked about Jeb not being here, so maybe she had been wrong after all. Then she gasped when she realized that Marie was off tonight.

"I will cut off his balls," she muttered. *Stop jumping to conclusions!*

"Hey, sugar, can I get a beer?"

Scarlett mentally groaned. She knew that voice. She was hoping the last time he was here would be the last time she ever saw him. She took a deep breath and turned to see Jayden Powers and his buddies sitting at the bar.

"Yes." She got him a beer and set it in front of him on the bar.

"Thanks, babe." He winked at her.

129

She leaned over the bar. "I am *not* your babe. Quit being a jerk, or I'll have you thrown out of here."

"Whoa, sugar, I was just thanking you."

"Leave her the fuck alone," Noah said from beside Powers, and Scarlett was shocked to see him here.

"Hell, not you, again. I'm getting tired of dealing with you."

Noah grinned. "Dealing with me? Is that what you call it? Do I need to remind you what happened the last time?"

"Back the fuck off, man. I'm just having a beer."

"Make sure that's all it is." Noah resumed his seat.

"That's some watchdog you have there, sugar." Powers got to his feet. "I'm probably better in bed, though."

Lord, she hoped he didn't cause more trouble. His buddies laughed as they all headed for a table. She spotted Deputy Mark Shaw making his rounds and called him over. She explained about Powers, and she was afraid he would cause problems again.

"I'll stick around a little while," Mark said, then moved through the crowd.

As the night wore on, Scarlett did her best to ignore Noah. She glanced over to see him watching her. He raised his beer bottle to her. She took a deep breath and headed for him.

"Do you want another beer?" she asked.

"Sure." He never took his eyes off her.

She walked to the cooler, slid the door open, removed another bottle, twisted the cap off, and

130

made her way back to him. She set it in front of him.

"Thanks," he said.

"You're welcome." She turned away then back to him. "Why are you here, Noah?"

"I can't come into the bar?"

"You know damn well what I mean. We don't see each other anymore, so why are you here?"

"Is it my fault we're not seeing each other? I didn't break it off. You did."

"Because I want more than you're willing to give," she snapped.

He pushed to his feet. "And I told you from the start how it was."

Scarlett watched him turn and weave through the crowd until the door opened, and he disappeared as he headed outside. Sighing, she picked up his untouched beer, poured it out in the sink, and tossed the bottle into the recycle bin, then turned to wait on other customers at the bar when she saw the group of young cowboys quickly heading toward the doors with Jayden Powers leading them. Scarlett looked over the crowd and spotted Mark.

"Mark," she called out as she waved her hand at him, and he came up to the bar.

"What's up?"

"Jayden Powers and those young cowboys just headed out the doors behind Noah."

"I got it." He turned and pushed through the crowd to head out. A few minutes passed, and she sighed with relief when she saw the group come back in with Mark behind them. He followed them to the table, and they all took their seats. He turned and headed back to the bar. "I told them they had to sit here until they were sober enough to drive. I'm going to head out, but I'll be back around. I know what vehicle they're in. I caught them right before they climbed into the truck, so if I see them gone or leaving, I'm going to pull them over. A sobriety test might be in order," he said with a grin.

Scarlett laughed. "I appreciate you, Mark. I'll let the servers know those boys are cut-off for the night."

"Yes, ma'am. Have a good evening. Call Paul or me if you have any more problems."

"I will. Thank you."

He touched the brim of his hat and walked out. Scarlett looked to the table to see the cowboys glaring at her. It was times like this that she was happy she lived above the bar. That group bought a lot of drinks tonight, so she was sure they were ready for some brawling. She didn't want them going after Noah. With five of them, she wasn't sure how it would go. She snorted. Noah would probably be able to handle all of them.

Sighing, she turned and filled some empty glasses, poured beer, or placed bottles in front of patrons. The six servers were keeping busy at the tables. Scarlett glanced at the clock to see it was almost one. Her feet were killing her, and the bed was calling her name. Too bad she hadn't asked Noah to stay, but she couldn't. She had broken it off with him, and she knew she couldn't risk getting involved with him again. It was over.

Blowing out a breath, she tilted her head down and blinked tears away. She raised her head and then waited on customers until she saw the time.

"Last call," she yelled out as she rang the big bell behind the bar. It was one, and she planned to be out of here by two-thirty, if possible. The band had packed up at midnight.

The bar was crowded tonight, and she was so glad tomorrow was Sunday. Well, today was, anyway. The servers came to the bar with orders, and Scarlett and the other two bartenders made the drinks or got beer for them.

As the last patrons left the bar, Scarlett followed the employees to the doors.

"Goodnight, everyone. See you Monday if you're scheduled. Enjoy your Sunday."

They all said goodnight to her, and she locked the doors behind them. With a big yawn, she walked through the bar, flipping out the lights, then headed for the door that led up to her apartment. She would clean the bar later, she thought as she slowly climbed the steps and regretted not asking Noah to go upstairs with her. She was such a fool where he was concerned, but she loved him so much. She also knew she couldn't ask him to stay with her anymore. She was going to marry Granger. *Who are you trying to convince?*

"Me. I'm trying to convince me," she whispered.

What a mess her life was. Who knew she would fall in love with one man and marry another? Why was she even considering it? She blew out a frustrated breath.

Shaking her head, she unlocked the door leading up to her apartment, climbed the steps, opened the door at the top of the stairs, and then locked it behind her.

She missed Noah so much. His touch. The way he could make her hot with just a look. She leaned back against the door, and the tears rolled down her face.

"You knew," she whispered. "You knew it would never go anywhere. He never lied to you. He had been honest from the start. You let your heart rule your head."

Friday night was even crazier than last weekend. Didn't these people have other things to do? Scarlett knew she shouldn't complain. It paid the bills. She set a mixed drink down in front of a woman, moved to the next person, and saw Noah sitting at the bar. She knew right then that she would spend the night with him. *One last time.*

She took a deep breath and walked over to where he sat, leaned her arms on the bar, and looked into his eyes. He raised an eyebrow at her.

"Stay with me tonight."

"What?"

"Isn't that why you keep coming back? You want to go upstairs with me."

"I'm not stupid, Scarlett. Of course, I want to stay with you, but you're going to marry another man."

Scarlett touched his hand. "I want you to stay, Noah. I'm not officially engaged. I mean, he hasn't put a ring on my finger yet." She held up her left hand, wriggled her fingers, and shrugged. God! She was going to be so embarrassed if he turned her down. She needed to be with him. *Once more.*

Noah continued to stare at her, then nodded.

"All right."

She smiled. "Good, and I'm happy to see that beard gone."

When the bar closed, she watched everyone file out except for Noah. He sat on the stool, staring at her. She took her apron off, tossed it onto the cooler, walked around the bar to the doors, and locked them. She walked to where he sat. He spun around on the stool, and she stepped between his thighs, reached up, removed his cowboy hat, and put it on her head. His hands went to her hips. He pulled her close, lowered his head, but hovered his lips above hers and stared into her eyes.

"Your move," he whispered.

She grinned, pressed her lips to his, and he took over, deepening the kiss. She moaned when his tongue moved into her mouth, and she touched hers to his.

Noah slowly raised his lips from hers. "Are you sure?"

"Yes, come on." She took his hand, led him through the bar, and up to her apartment.

They had barely stepped inside when he grabbed her and slammed his lips down on hers. He lifted her, and she wrapped her legs around his waist. She could feel his hard cock against her.

"I believe you want me, Noah Conway," she whispered when she pulled her lips from his.

"I do."

"Then take me to bed." She removed his hat from her head and tossed it to the sofa as he carried her to the bedroom.

He let her down, shrugged his coat off, let it

fall to the floor, and pulled his T-shirt off. Scarlett removed her clothes, then crawled onto the bed and watched him strip off his jeans and boxer briefs. She groaned when she saw his hard cock standing up. He bent down, removed his wallet from his jeans, and took out a condom.

After he placed the wallet on the nightstand, he sheathed himself, got on the bed next to her, and pressed his lips to hers again. His lips slid across her cheek to her ear, down to her neck, and lower to her breasts. She raked her fingers through his thick hair.

When he sucked a nipple into his mouth, she arched against him. His lips moved to the other one, then he moved down her stomach to the juncture of her thighs, spread her legs with his shoulders, pulled her slit apart with his thumbs, and sucked on her until she cried out as she came.

He moved back up to her lips and kissed them, and she could taste herself on his lips.

"Noah," she whispered.

"Tell me, Scarlett. Tell me what you want," he demanded.

"I want you to fuck me. Now, please," she pleaded, then gasped when he thrust hard into her. She wrapped her legs around his waist as he pounded into her, and it wasn't long before she knew she was going over again. She screamed his name as he grunted and came with her.

After a few minutes of trying to catch their breaths, they took a shower and fell asleep, but she woke him up later when she started sucking on his dick. She wanted to give him a night he would never forget. He moaned in his sleep then woke up.

"Scarlett," he groaned.

"Tell me, Noah. Tell me what you want," she threw his words back at him.

"I want you to come up here and straddle me. Ride me, baby," he said through clenched teeth

"Anything for you," she said as she crawled up his body, pressed her lips to his, and lowered herself onto him. She started to move herself up and down his length but stopped when he put his hands on her hips to stop her. She looked down at him to see him looking up at her.

"Get a condom," he said through clenched teeth.

"I'm on birth control. This time, we're going to go skin on skin. Please, Noah. I'm safe, and I know you are. You always wear a condom."

"I am." He closed his eyes and nodded.

Scarlett rode him until his hand moved between them, and he moved his thumb against her clitoris, throwing her over. Then a guttural groan tore from him as he came. She collapsed onto his chest then rolled to lay beside him. She would forever love this man.

"I'm still marrying Granger," she whispered.

****

Later that night, Noah opened his eyes, and it took him a minute to realize where he was. Scarlett had her head on his chest, and he raised his head to kiss the top of her head. She moaned in her sleep, and his dick shot up. God, he loved being with her, but he just couldn't give her what she wanted. Blowing out a breath, he frowned as he thought about her saying earlier that she was

137

still going to marry Crawford. Then why be in bed with him now? He lightly shook her to wake her.

"What?" she asked in a sleepy voice.

"Why are we here?"

"What do you mean?" She pushed against his chest and sat up.

Reaching up, he tucked her hair behind her ear.

"You told me you were still marrying Crawford. So why are we here?"

"I wanted to be with you again, Noah. One last time before I marry Granger."

He scooted up against the headboard and narrowed his eyes.

"What the hell does that mean, Scarlett? I'm just good for a fuck once in a while?" He watched as she threw the sheet off, got out of the bed, grabbed her robe, and pulled it on, and turned to look at him.

"Isn't that all I am to you?" she asked as she tied the belt around the robe.

Noah blew out a frustrated breath as he tossed the sheet off, got up from the bed, found his boxer briefs and jeans, and pulled them on. He sat on the edge of the bed, pulled on his socks and boots, then stood to stomp his feet into them.

"Noah," she snapped.

He tugged his T-shirt over his head and spun around. "What?"

Scarlett stalked to him, stopped in front of him, and stared up at him.

"Answer me. Isn't that all I am to you?"

"You know damn well you're not—"

"But yet, you can't commit to me." She placed

her hands on her hips.

"Damn it, Scarlett. I don't see anyone but you. Isn't that commitment?"

"That's not what I mean, and you know it. I want more. I want to get married, have kids. You don't."

"So again, *why are we here*?" he asked through clenched teeth.

"I suppose because I'm a fool for you." She flopped down onto the side of the bed. "I'm twenty-nine years old, Noah. I want a family, and I don't want to be too old to enjoy them. You don't want that."

Sighing, he took a seat beside her and took her hand in his.

"Scarlett, you knew that going in. I have had my heart stepped on and broken more than any man deserves."

"I wouldn't do that."

Noah blew out a humorless laugh. "Yeah, I've heard that before."

"I don't know how to convince you." She sighed. "I'd never hurt you."

"Never say never, darlin'." He felt like an ass when a tear rolled down her cheek. He shot to his feet. "I'm leaving. This sure wasn't how I wanted this night to go. You want what I can't give you." He raked his fingers through his hair. "As much as I hate to admit it, Crawford can."

"I wouldn't hurt you," she repeated.

"I've heard it before," he snapped.

"Not from me," she shouted.

"Scarlett, look, I don't want you to marry him, but we're at a standstill here. Why can't we just continue the way we are?"

"What about kids?"

"We could have them..."

"Bullshit, Noah." Scarlett shook her head. "You need to leave."

Huffing out a breath, he leaned down, kissed the top of her head, picked up his coat, shrugged it on, strode to the living room, got his hat from the sofa, slapped it on his head, and stepped out the door that led outside. He pulled the door closed behind him and practically ran down the metal stairs.

Striding around the building, he clenched his jaw as he headed for his truck. Pointing the fob at it, the lights flashed, and the horn chirped. He opened the door, climbed inside, then tore out of the parking lot.

Chapter Seven

"Why the hell do you keep going in there?" Noah asked himself as he drove home.

Nothing but a heartache every time he went into that bar and saw her. She would marry Crawford, even though she had sex with *him*. How would Crawford feel if he knew the woman he would marry slept with another man? He knew he'd never tell him. As Scarlett said, they weren't officially engaged...

"But she told you she was going to marry him. Fuck," he shouted.

When he pulled up to his house, the sun was beginning to rise. He stopped the truck and sat there staring out the windshield. He could see that he wouldn't get a thing done today. Damn her. Damn her for getting him back in bed. He should have known better.

"You had to have her, you fucking idiot."

He jerked when someone tapped on the window, and he looked over to the passenger side to see Brad standing there. Noah put the window down.

"You just getting home?" Brad asked with a grin.

"Yes," he growled out and watched the grin leave Brad's face.

"Uh, oh. So, not a good night, huh?"

"Oh, the night was good, just not the morning." Noah raised the window then stepped out of the truck.

"I won't ask."

"Good, because I wouldn't tell you anyway."

"Damn, Noah. You're in a piss poor mood this morning."

"Yeah, and it's not going to get better as the day goes on." He walked up the steps, opened the door, and looked back at Brad. "I'll be in here all fucking day if you need me." He stepped inside and slammed the door.

****

There were some nights Scarlett questioned her sanity on buying the bar. It was beyond packed for a Friday night. Even people on the dance floor were having a hard time moving around. The band was cranking out the songs, but no one could dance to them. Shaking her head, she watched as Laura waited on people along the bar, and she got busy helping her.

As she served a beer to a cowboy, she noticed Jayden Powers and his buddies sitting at a table. Why couldn't they stay out of here? She could refuse to serve them, but she was sure that would just cause more problems. When Powers saw her looking his way, he winked at her, and she turned her back to him. He gave her the creeps. He always seemed to be up to no good.

She tried to keep an eye on him and his buddies, but the bar was so packed that she couldn't because she was just too busy. Laura was buzzing around too. Scarlett glanced around the bar and saw Jeb sitting in his usual spot. Of course, he was. Marie was working tonight.

"You have to stop making assumptions," she muttered.

"What?"

Scarlett glanced over to see Marie standing

142

beside her.

"I was talking to myself."

"Oh, okay." Marie turned to walk away.

"Marie?"

"Yes," she said as she turned back to look at Scarlett.

"I've never asked. Do you have a boyfriend?"

Marie looked startled by the question.

"Uh, no."

"Why not? You're a pretty, young woman."

"I'm not interested in a steady one right now."

"I see. I'm sure you will be one day. Can I offer you some advice?" At Marie's nod, Scarlett went on. "Just make sure you don't fuck around with another woman's man. It never ends well."

She watched as Marie's eyes widened, then she nodded, picked up some drinks, and headed for a table. Scarlett grinned. She hoped Marie got the message. Scarlett wanted her to know she suspected something, and by the look on the woman's face, Scarlett was right, but she still wasn't sure enough to where she could tell Laura anything. *If* there were a chance she was wrong, she'd lose Laura. Not only as a bartender but as a friend, and she didn't want to lose her as either. She knew Laura wouldn't work for her if she accused Jeb of cheating on her and found out she was wrong.

Huffing out a breath, she got back to serving drinks, but her thoughts ran to Noah. She hadn't heard from him, but she hadn't expected to. Their last night together had been amazing, but it would never happen again. Two weeks had passed, and he hadn't been back to the bar or called her.

The hardest thing she did was tell Granger about being with Noah that night...

"I'm so sorry," she said as tears rolled down her face.

"Scarlett, I know you love him. I'm surprised it didn't happen sooner. I understand if you don't want to marry me. I honestly do," Granger said.

"I want to get married to you, Granger. I think we can make a go of it, and I swear to you that it will never happen again. Noah knows I'm marrying you. I told him that night. If you still want to marry me, that is."

"Of course, I do, but if he changes his mind and wants to marry you, I won't stand in your way."

Scarlett shook her head. "He won't."

Granger wrapped his arms around her. "I'm so sorry, hon."

She had wept on his shoulder until she was sure she had no tears left. He was such a good man and deserved someone a hell of a lot better than her.

As she listened to the band, she smiled when they started playing *I Love This Bar*, a song by Toby Keith. She laughed out loud when the crowd sang along. As she served drinks and filled the baskets with peanuts and pretzels, she turned to see Granger sitting at the bar. Smiling, she made her way to him, leaned her arms on the bar, and stared at him. He was a very good-looking man, and she was sure it wouldn't be such a hardship being married to him.

"What are you doing here?"

"I wanted to come back and see you. I had to go back home for a while."

Scarlett straightened up. "Just what are we supposed to do about that, Granger?"

"What do you mean?"

"I just bought this bar. I don't want to leave here."

"We'll have to figure something out, Scarlett. I have a law practice in Missoula."

"I know, but I have a bar *here*," she said.

"I get it. We'll figure it out. Can I get a beer? Whatever's on tap is fine."

"Sure." She walked to the cooler, removed a frosted mug, held it under the tap, and filled it. She couldn't stop thinking about how they'd make this work and why she hadn't thought of it before. Mentally shaking her head, she knew they would have to figure it out because she would not sell. There was no way she was leaving Clifton or her bar. It had been a dream of hers to own a bar, and she finally achieved it.

She set the mug down in front of him and smiled when he smiled at her. *How was this going to work?*

"Hey," Granger said.

"Yeah?"

"We'll get through it."

"I hope we can because I'm not leaving this bar behind."

Granger's lips tightened as he got to his feet.

"Not leaving this bar, or not leaving Conway?"

Scarlett gasped. "Do not start with me, Granger."

"Why not, Scarlett? You could sell this bar and buy one in Missoula. I'm not so sure it's the bar that's keeping you here." He reached for his wallet, pulled out cash, and paid for his beer.

Then he turned and walked out of the bar.

"Damn it," she muttered as she picked up the mug of his untouched beer.

"Who was that?"

Scarlett glanced from the door to her side to see Laura.

"That was Granger."

"Wow, he's good-looking. What happened?"

"I'll tell you later." Scarlett looked along the bar. "We're too busy now."

"All right." Laura turned to wait on patrons.

When Scarlett rang the bell and yelled that it was last call, she was more than ready to hit the sheets. Her feet hurt. She was tired and had one hell of a headache.

Once the bar cleared out, she walked around the tables picking up empty bottles and glasses. She looked over to see Laura doing the same. They were the only two in the place. Scarlett pulled a chair out from a table and plopped down onto it. Laura set the bottles on the bar, walked to the table, pulled a chair out, and took a seat.

"Tell me." Laura leaned her arms on the table.

Scarlett shook her head and told Laura about the conversation with Granger.

"Is he right?" Laura asked her.

"I don't know. I honestly don't, Laura." She looked at her. "Am I holding onto this bar as an excuse to be near Noah?"

"Only you can answer that, Scarlett."

She shook her head. "I miss him so damn much. I'll never love anyone as much as I love him. I know that much. Poor Granger doesn't deserve that. That man needs a good woman in his life, not one in love with another man."

146

"The way I see it is if you want to make a life with Granger, then maybe you do need to sell the bar and leave Clifton...and Noah behind."

"Easier said than done, my friend. Easier said than done. I was so sure I could marry Granger, but Noah and I spent the night together—"

Laura sat up. "What? When?"

"Two weeks ago. I knew I shouldn't have, but I asked him to stay with me for the night. I told myself it would be just one more time, but if that man walked in the door right now and wanted to take me to bed, I'd go willingly. Why is love so hard? Why did I have to fall for a man who never wants to settle down?"

"You mean who wants to get married. Did he ever say he wouldn't settle down?"

Scarlett frowned. "What difference does it make?"

Laura shrugged. "Some people will settle down but not get married. Look at Kurt Russell and Goldie Hawn. They've been together for years but never married."

"Noah always said he never wanted to get married, and he did mention us continuing on the way we were, but when I asked him about kids, he said we could have them. I know many people live together as man and wife without a marriage license, and I applaud them for that, but I don't want that. I want to get married."

"If you say so, but if you're going to marry Granger, then you might have to sell the bar and move to Missoula."

"I don't want to go back to Missoula. I love Clifton and my bar—"

"And Noah," Laura added.

Scarlett huffed out a breath. "I just don't know what to do."

"You love Noah. How can you marry another man?"

"I want kids, Laura. I want to get married."

Laura sighed. "I know you do, but marrying a man you don't love will eventually cause problems, and you and Granger will end up divorced." She touched Scarlett's hand. "I know you don't want to hurt him, but you will if you go through with this. As you said, Granger doesn't deserve that."

Scarlett pushed to her feet. "I think I'll clean this up tomorrow. Go home to Jeb, Laura. I'll see you tomorrow night."

"All right. I'll see you then." Laura hugged her then disappeared down the hall. She came back out wearing her coat and beanie. She waved at her and walked out.

Scarlett locked the doors, turned the lights out, and climbed the stairs to her apartment. After locking the door, she headed for her bedroom and wiped tears from her cheeks.

"Damn you, Noah Conway. Why in the hell did you ever come into my life?"

****

Noah wiped the saddle down, picked it up, and carried it to the room where he kept the finished ones. He had finished this one in record time. He was out here all hours of the night since he didn't sleep. He couldn't because he saw Scarlett every time he closed his eyes. He wondered if he ever crossed her mind. Damn, he missed her.

He walked out of the room and headed down the barn aisle. He opened the barn door and shook his head when he saw it was snowing again.

Heading for the porch, he glanced behind him and saw that the horses weren't in the corral. As he walked up the steps, he pulled his cellphone from his coat pocket and called Brad.

"Where are the horses?" he asked when Brad answered.

"We're bringing them in. I was sure we'd have them in before you finished for the day."

"I finished the saddle I was working on and heading in when I noticed they weren't in the corral."

"You're done that saddle already?"

Noah could hear the surprise in Brad's voice.

"Yeah, I worked on it all day and night."

"Hell, Noah, just marry the damn woman," Brad snapped and disconnected.

Noah wiped his feet on the mat, opened the door, set the phone on the table then removed his hat and coat.

After hanging them up, he picked up the phone and headed for the living room. He strode to the fireplace, opened the flue, and lit a match to the wood. He took a seat in the recliner and watched the flames wrap around the wood as it snapped and crackled.

No one knew how he felt unless they went through it as he had. Women were so damn hard to understand, but damn, he loved them and respected them. Particularly a certain redhead, but he was too damn chicken to take another chance and especially with her.

As bad as he hurt right now not having her, he knew he would want to crawl into a ball and die if they were to get engaged, and she'd break it off, and she would. Of that, he had no doubt. It was just the way his luck went with women.

He lifted the footrest, leaned back, and closed his eyes. His ass was dragging. He needed some sleep. Since it was Friday, maybe he'd be lucky and sleep until Monday.

****

Saturday afternoon, Scarlett needed to make a trip to town to get some necessities. As she drove past the diner, her stomach growled, and she had to pull into the parking lot because those burgers were calling her name.

Tess Garrett had told her how good the burgers were in the little restaurant. Scarlett had her doubts until she tasted one.

After parking, she stepped from her SUV and walked to the door. She opened it, and the bell above the door announced her. She chuckled when people inside waved or called out to her. Mentally shaking her head, she made her way to an empty stool at the counter and took a seat.

"Hey, Scarlett."

She looked up to see Deidra Mitchell standing on the opposite side of the counter, holding a coffee carafe. Scarlett nodded for her to fill the cup.

"Hey, Deidra. How are you doing?"

"I'm great. Would you like your usual?"

Scarlett laughed. "I have no idea how you remember what it is."

Deidra leaned forward. "I don't, but Uncle Owen will know." Deidra winked. "I don't know how he or Aunt Connie remember everyone's usual, but they do."

"It shocked me the first time Connie asked me, and I thought there was no way she could remember, but damn if she didn't."

"Those two are the best."

"They are. I'll have my usual then, Deidra. Thank you." Scarlett smiled.

"You're welcome. It will be just a few minutes. We're not that busy." Deidra wrote on the pad.

"Just what do you write on that pad for Owen if you don't know what the usual is?" Scarlett asked as she tilted her head.

Deidra grinned. "I wrote, Scarlett's usual, on it."

Scarlett laughed as Deidra walked to the pass-through window, pinned the order to the metal wheel then spun it around for Owen. The bell above the door chimed, and she glanced over to see Rayna Dillon enter, holding a little girl's hand, and a man entered behind her. She had met Rayna when she'd been with the group of women at the bar one night. She smiled when Rayna spotted her.

"Scarlett, how are you?" Rayna asked her as she let go of the little girl's hand and hugged her.

"I'm great, Rayna. Who is this pretty little girl?" She smiled when the little girl hid her face against the man's jeans-clad legs behind Rayna. Scarlett looked up at him and went dumbstruck because he was devastatingly handsome.

"This is Harlee Dillon and her daddy, Trick. My husband. Trick, Harlee, this is Scarlett Robinson," Rayna said with a grin.

"It's nice to meet you both." Scarlett put her hand out to Harlee, who giggled and placed her hand in hers. Scarlett looked up at Trick and

151

mentally groaned. "Hello, Trick."

"Scarlett," he said in a deep voice as he touched the brim of his hat and looked at Rayna. "We'll grab a booth, darlin'."

Scarlett watched him kiss Rayna's temple, pick up Harlee, weave his way through the tables, and get stopped by people as he headed to a booth. She looked back to Rayna.

"Wow," was all she said, but Rayna laughed.

"I know. The first time I saw him, I almost fell out of my saddle. Hey, I'd better get going. I'll see you on the next girl's night out." Rayna hugged her again and headed back to the booth where Trick and Harlee sat.

Scarlett watched as Trick slid out when Rayna reached him then sat again once she was seated. Some men still had manners.

A few minutes later, Deidra set her lunch before her, and she dug in. The food here was fantastic. As she sat there eating, she wondered what Noah was doing. Not Granger, the man she was going to marry, but Noah, the man who didn't want her. She set her burger back on the plate as her appetite left her. Damn that man. Why did she ever get involved with him?

A little while later, she paid for her meal and walked outside to see snow flurries. It wasn't accumulating, but as she looked to the Glacier Mountains in the distance, she couldn't see the tops and knew from experience that meant more snow was coming. She quickly made her way along the sidewalk to get her shopping done and head home. Since it was Saturday, she needed to get back and get ready for the crowd tonight at the bar. If the snow didn't amount to much, she knew it would be packed.

At seven that evening, she glanced around to see it was way more than packed. It was wall-to-wall people. The snow had arrived, but no one seemed to mind. She shook her head and knew that people would be at Dewey's unless the snow made the roads impassable.

As she served a cowboy a beer, she glanced to the door when it opened and flattened her lips when she saw Jayden Powers and his bunch saunter through the crowd. He looked over at her, touched the brim of his hat, and they made their way to a table. Scarlett was hoping there weren't any available, but they found one.

A few minutes later, she saw a raised hand along the bar and walked to the person, only to stop in her tracks when she saw Powers sitting there grinning at her.

"What can I get you?" she asked.

"You know you could get some better servers. We've been sitting there a little while, and no one has waited on us," he said with a smirk.

"Do you see how busy we are?" she snapped.

"Whoa, darlin', I was just commenting."

"What can I get you?" she repeated.

He gave her his order, and she turned to get it. She wished he would stop coming in here. She trusted him about as far as she could throw him. Turning back to him, she set the beer bottles in front of him on the bar then noticed when a deputy walked by, and Powers turned away from him. She didn't know the deputy; it wasn't Nevada, Mark, Brody, or Paul.

Powers paid for the beer, picked up the bottles then made his way back to the table. Scarlett frowned. Why had he turned away from that deputy when he hadn't from the other deputies?

She glanced around for the deputy and saw him heading back toward her, but several people stopped him and spoke with him. When he turned back her way, she was again struck by how good-looking a lot of men were in this town. He was very tall, with dark brown, almost black hair, and even from here, she could see his gorgeous blue eyes. He spotted her looking at him, and her cheeks flamed. He made his way to the bar and grinned at her. She was sure her mouth was hanging open.

"Ma'am," he said, touching the brim of his hat. "We haven't met. I'm Sheriff Sam Garrett."

"You're Tess's husband," Scarlett exclaimed, and his grin widened.

"Yes, ma'am. Are you Scarlett?"

"I am." She stuck her hand over the bar, and he shook it.

"It's nice to meet you. Tessa told me you bought the bar from Dewey. She loves her girls' night out here."

"They have a good time," Scarlett said with a laugh.

The sheriff shook his head. "That they do. I was on my way home. Late night at the office. I just thought I'd stop in. I'm sure Nevada and Paul will be by later."

"Nevada? Where's Mark?"

"He's on vacation this week. Nevada took his shift." He touched the brim of his hat. "You have a good night, Scarlett."

"I'll try, Sheriff."

"Sam, please. Call if you need us," he said,

turned, and headed for the door.

Damn. Tess was one lucky woman. Scarlett smiled as she watched Sam try to make it to the door, but people kept stopping him to talk. When he finally reached it, it opened, and the smile left her face when she saw Noah enter. He stopped to talk to Sam for a few minutes. Then they shook hands, and Sam walked out. Noah made his way to the bar and took a seat on a stool.

She should ignore him, but he was a customer, so she made her way to him.

"What can I get you, Noah?"

"Callahan and Coke," he said.

She raised an eyebrow. "Hitting the hard stuff tonight, aren't you?"

"Why should that bother you?" His lips flattened.

Scarlett shrugged. "It doesn't. Drink until you pass out for all I care."

"Best idea you've ever had," he muttered, but she heard him.

She leaned over the bar. "Yeah, I've had some bad ones lately."

"No shit, Scarlett."

Turning, she blinked her eyes quickly and made him his drink, then took it back to him. She set it on a napkin then moved away from him. She could smell his aftershave, and she hated that it brought back memories of putting her face against his neck and inhaling.

"Son of a bitch," she muttered.

"Are you all right with him here?" Laura asked her.

"Yes, but could you wait on him for however long he's here?"

"Of course." Laura touched her arm.

Scarlett nodded, moved along the bar, and refilled drinks. This night could not end soon enough.

****

Noah watched her wait on everyone but him. That woman was the most hardheaded person he had ever met. He supposed she was sending him a message. It was over, and she was going to marry Crawford.

"Motherfucker," he murmured as he lifted his glass to take a sip.

He rarely drank hard liquor, but he knew he needed it tonight. He needed the courage to tell her he didn't want her marrying Crawford. Yeah, he knew he had told her before, but this time he had to convince her she belonged with him, not Crawford. Why couldn't she see that?

"Hey, Noah."

He glanced over to see Jeb taking a seat beside him and nodded at him.

"Jeb."

Out of the corner of his eye, he saw Jeb raise his hand to get a bartender's attention. He saw Scarlett tighten her jaw then walk to where they sat.

"What can I get you, Jeb?"

"Beer is fine. Whatever's on tap, Scarlett."

"I'll be right back."

"What's with her tonight?" Jeb asked him.

"Who knows?"

"Laura told me she was marrying some guy...shit, I forget his name."

"Granger Crawford," Noah growled out.

"And you're going to let her?"

156

Noah turned on the stool to face Jeb.

"I can't tell her what to do," he snapped.

"Hell, Noah, don't bite my head off. I just thought you and Scarlett would stay together."

"Yeah, well, that won't happen." He spun back to face the bar.

"I see."

"Do you, Jeb?"

"Now, what's with *your* attitude?" Jeb said.

"Let me tell you something, Jeb. More people see things in here than you realize." Noah looked at him and narrowed his eyes. He watched Jeb raise an eyebrow.

"I have no idea what that means."

Noah blew out a laugh. "You just keep telling yourself that."

Jeb didn't say another word, and Noah was glad about that because he was in the mood to punch someone, and Jeb was right here. Noah picked up his glass, tossed the drink back, and raised his hand, but Laura was busy. He mentally grinned when Scarlett walked to him.

"Refill?"

"Yes."

She reached for his glass, and he wrapped his fingers around her wrist, making her stop to look at him.

"What is it, Noah?"

"Can we talk?"

"There is nothing to talk about. You made your choice, and I've made mine." She jerked her arm away from him and walked away with his glass. When she brought the drink back, she set it down then moved along the bar.

Shit. He didn't have a snowball's chance in

157

hell of getting her to listen to him. He just wanted to let her know that he wanted her back in his life. He shook his head. She didn't want him, though. Well, too damn bad if she didn't want to listen to him. He was sticking around until everyone was gone after closing. She would have to listen then. He would leave if she didn't want to and never come back.

****

Scarlett looked at the clock and rang the bell for last call. An hour later, she glanced around to see that the bar had finally emptied, except for Noah. He sat at the bar watching her, but she shook her head and watched as he got to his feet, turned, and strode to the doors leading outside. He put his hand hard against the push bar, and the door flew open.

Once he disappeared, she walked to the door to lock it up for the night. As she put the key into the deadbolt, she looked out the window in the door to watch him walk to his truck, and out of the corner of her eye, she saw five cowboys heading toward him. When one of them glanced to the bar, she gasped as she recognized Jayden Powers.

Pushing against the door, she ran outside.

"Noah!" she shouted, making him turn around.

One of Powers' friends hit Noah across the back with a bat, and he fell to the ground. Another one kicked him. Scarlett ran toward them, screaming for them to stop.

"Get that bitch and take her back inside. Help me get him up. We'll all just go into the bar. Safer that way." Powers sneered.

Scarlett screamed and ran back toward the bar, but two of the cowboys grabbed her. She kicked and slapped at them, but one caught her legs, and the other picked her up by her arms, and they carried her inside.

"Sit her down at one of the tables. Pull a chair out for this prick," Powers shouted out orders.

"What do you plan to do?" Scarlett asked.

"I'm going to kick the shit out of this fucker, and then we're going to have a little fun with you," Powers said with a sadistic grin.

"Good thing you brought back up because you can't take me on by yourself, you gutless pussy," Noah said, then grunted when Powers hit him in the face while two of his friends held him.

Scarlett watched as Noah spit blood out of his mouth, narrowed his eyes at Powers, and grinned.

"Let's do this man to man. You said you weren't a boy, but you sure are acting like one."

"I'm going to show your woman how much of a man I am when I'm finished with you."

"You touch one hair on her head, and I will fucking kill you," Noah said in a low menacing voice.

Powers walked to him, punched him in the gut, making him grunt and fall to his knees.

"Did that hurt? A big man like you can't take a punch to the gut?"

"Let go of me, and I'll show you what I can take. You chicken shit little prick," Noah said between clenched teeth.

"You know, we've been waiting for this. To get you both at the same time." Powers turned to Scarlett. "I didn't believe you the night you said he was upstairs. That's why we left. You shouldn't have turned me down, babe, and this prick here should have minded his own fucking business." He kicked Noah, sending him onto his back.

"Stop it," Scarlett shouted.

Powers turned, walked to her, leaned down, and looked into her face.

"I'm going to take my time with you," he said, making her shudder.

"What's that for you? About fifteen seconds?" She gasped when he slapped her face.

"You're no man if you hit a woman." She spat blood out from her busted lip.

"I like it rough," Powers said with a grin, then looked at his friends. "Get him up and put him in a chair. He can watch while I have his woman."

Scarlett watched them lift Noah to a chair. His eyes were closed, and a bruise was already forming on his cheek.

"Please," she whispered.

Powers turned to look at her. "Oh, now you're going to plead with me, huh? Do you care about him that much? Let me tell you something, sugar. He's like any other man. He wants that pussy, but by the time I'm done with you, he won't ever touch you again."

"Why are you doing this?" Scarlett looked up at him with tears in her eyes.

"Because you turned me down, and he butted in."

"He stood up to you for talking to me the way you did. I turned you down because you sure as shit don't appeal to me. Probably the only way

160

you can get a woman is by force."

Powers laughed. "You're gonna find out."

"He's not even my man anymore. I'm going to marry someone else," Scarlett said.

"Yeah, like I'd fall for that," Powers snapped.

"It's true. She broke it off with me," Noah said and spat more blood out.

Powers shook his head. "You two will say anything to stop this." He looked at his friends. "Let go of him."

"Are you nuts?" one of them asked.

"Let him go." Powers reached into the front pocket of his jeans, pulled out a knife, and snapped the blade open with a flick of his wrist. "I got this."

"Stop it," Scarlett yelled.

"You're next, sugar. Right after we all have a little fun with you, you'll be wondering why you did turn me down."

"That would be the only way you'd ever have me."

Powers turned to look at her. "Do you think that bothers me?"

"You're a disgusting pig," she spat at him.

He strode to her and slapped her across the face again, and then he turned just in time to see Noah running at him.

She watched as the blade sunk into Noah and the surprise on his face when it did. He grunted, fell to his knees, and then to the floor on his stomach.

"Noah," she shouted.

"It's time to have a little fun. It's just too bad he won't be around to watch." Powers sneered as he looked at her and waved the blade in front of her.

Two of his buddies held her while he slid the knife up under her T-shirt and sliced it open. Then he put the blade against her bra, and with a grin, cut it and used the knife to move the material aside.

"Nice tits," he said as he slid the tip of the blade around her nipple.

Scarlett slammed her knee up into his groin, making him grunt, fall to his knees and grab his crotch.

"You fucking whore," he groaned out, and she could hear the pain in his voice.

"You sick little asshole. I will fight you tooth and nail," she said between clenched teeth.

"I like it that way," Powers said as he slowly got to his feet. He walked to her and put his hand on her breast. He started to lean down but spun around when the bar door crashed open.

"Drop the knife. Now," Nevada yelled as he entered, holding his weapon out in front of him. "You two let her go."

Scarlett whimpered with relief when she was let go. Without even thinking of her naked breasts, she ran to where Noah lay.

"You can't take on five of us," Powers said as he tossed the knife back and forth in his hands.

"Maybe not, but I sure as hell can get you first," Nevada said, all the while pointing his gun at Powers.

"We just might find out," Powers said as he jerked his chin for his friends to circle Nevada.

Scarlett looked up to see Nevada grin. "I've been in law enforcement for over twelve years. Do you think I can't take more than one of you out before you get to me? Try me." He tilted his head. "I'd say I could get, at least, three of you. So, who's it going to be? How faithful are your friends? How many are willing to take a bullet for you?"

She saw Powers' friends stop then back up to where Powers stood.

"Get back over there," he shouted at his friends, but none of them moved.

Scarlett couldn't believe it when Nevada walked to Powers and put the tip of the barrel of his weapon against his forehead.

"Drop that fucking knife now, or I will split your head wide open," he growled out. She sighed with relief when Powers dropped the knife.

Nevada backed away from him and motioned for them all to take a seat. Once they did, he kneeled beside Noah, put two fingers to his neck without taking his eyes off the group. Scarlett looked at Nevada with pleading eyes.

"He has a faint pulse. The ambulance is on the way." He straightened up, and she watched him remove his khaki shirt, then he placed it around her shoulders.

"Thank you. How did you know what was going on here?" She slid her arms through the shirt and buttoned it.

"I was doing the rounds and noticed the bar lights on. I know they're usually out by two-thirty, and when they weren't, I knew something was up. I parked, snuck up to the doors, and looked inside. I called Paul, Brody, and Sam for backup and an ambulance," Nevada said.

"I could kiss you, Nevada," she told him as

163

Sam and Paul came running inside the bar with Brody Morgan.

Deputy Paul Dixon handcuffed Powers and his friends. He had gotten Sam's and Nevada's handcuffs too. Now she knew why some cops carried more than one set. Brody stood holding his weapon out in front of him as the men were cuffed.

Scarlett got to her feet when two EMTs came into the bar with a stretcher. She put her hand over her mouth as she watched them roll Noah to his back, and his shirt was soaked with blood.

"If he dies, all five of you will be charged with first-degree murder...right after I kick the hell out of you. This man is a friend of mine." Sam glared at the young cowboys then looked at her. "You will press charges, right?"

Scarlett glanced at the young men. "Yes."

"Good. I'm sure everything was caught on your cameras. Nevada, Paul, take four of them in. I'll bring in Powers. Book them for attempted murder as of now, and assault. Brody, you can head back home. I appreciate you coming in."

"No problem, Sam." Brody looked at her and touched the brim of his hat. "Scarlett."

"Let's go," Nevada said as he grabbed two of them by their arms and led them outside. Paul took the other two. She could hear their rights being read to them. Powers sat at a table with his head down.

Noah was placed on the stretcher, and IVs were hooked up. He looked so pale.

"Will he live?" she croaked out.

"Not sure, ma'am. It will depend on if any vital organs were damaged. He's lost a lot of blood, though. Do you want to ride with us?"

"I'll be behind you. I need to change clothes, and...wash off."

"Take your time, Scarlett. I'll be at the hospital right after I book this little prick," Sam said as he pulled Powers to his feet, reading him his rights.

"Sam, wait." Scarlett walked up to Powers and slapped his face as hard as possible, making her hand sting, then looked at Sam. "You can take him now."

"You going to let her do that?" Powers asked Sam.

"Do what?" Sam winked at Scarlett.

"You son of a bitch," Powers snapped at Sam.

"That's *Sheriff* son of a bitch to you, asshole," he said as he jerked his arm and led him outside.

Scarlett locked the doors behind them, then ran through the bar and up to her apartment.

"Please, God. Please don't let him die," she said as tears rolled down her face.

Chapter Eight

Noah blinked his eyes against the bright lights and glanced around the room. He was in the hospital. *Damn, did the lights need to be this fucking bright?* For a minute, he couldn't remember what had happened to put him here, then he tried to sit up, and pain ripped through him.

"Stay down, Mr. Conway," a female voice said.

Noah grabbed his side and felt a bandage.

"Motherfucker, that hurt," he said between breaths.

"Well, you lost a lot of blood, and the wound was deep. It's going to hurt for a while. You're lucky to be alive," a nurse said as she checked his IV bag.

"Scarlett? Where's Scarlett?"

"I don't know who that is, but I can check for you. I wasn't here when you were brought in."

"When was that?"

"You've been here three days."

"Three days?"

"Yes, you've been in and out of consciousness. Your doctor is on his way. You can ask him any questions you have. Can I get you anything?"

"Just information on Scarlett Robinson. Please."

"I'll see what I can do. Do you need something for the pain?"

Noah hated taking pain meds, but the pain was unbearable, so he nodded. He watched as she took a syringe from her pocket and inserted it into the tubing. Within a few minutes, he was feeling no pain at all.

He tried to sit up the next day, but it was still painful. He was hungry, so he had to move the back of the bed up. Even though he wasn't given the best food, he ate. Yesterday had been a blur, and he hadn't seen his doctor yet. He wanted to know if Scarlett was all right. Dear God, if she was dead, he'd hunt down those little pricks and kill them one by one with his bare hands.

He glanced up and saw his sister enter the room. Hailey walked to him and hugged him.

"You scared the hell out of me, Noah," she whispered into his ear.

"Sorry, kiddo. I'm fine."

"You weren't. You lost a lot of blood." She straightened up and took hold of his hand.

He looked over to the door to see Gage enter the room.

"Well, you look better than you did," Gage said as he walked to the bed and shook his hand.

"I hope I look better than I feel," Noah said with a smirk.

"We were so worried," his mother said as she entered the room with his father behind her.

"I'm okay, Mom," he said.

"You could have died, son," his father commented as he stood at the end of the bed.

"I know—"

A man in a white coat entered his room and picked up a chart. After looking over it, he hung it back onto the bed and looked at him.

"Mr. Conway, you're a lucky man. The stab wound missed all your vital organs. You're damn lucky to be alive because you did lose a lot of blood."

"Where's Scarlett?"

"I don't know who she is. Is that your wife?"

"No," he said and knew right then that she should be.

"Scarlett is probably at the bar, Noah," Hailey told him.

"I need to get out of here," he muttered, then huffed out a relieved breath and blinked tears from his eyes because Scarlett was all right.

"You'll do no such thing, Noah."

He looked to the doorway to see Sam standing there.

"Sam, they could have killed us both."

"I know. They're in custody."

"How?"

"Luckily for you and Scarlett, Nevada was driving by around two-thirty and saw the bar lights still on. He said he had a gut feeling something wasn't right since any other night they were out at that time. He parked the cruiser, made his way to the window in the door, and looked in. He saw Powers stab you and head for Scarlett. He called for backup and went inside. Paul, Brody, and I got there as quickly as possible, but Nevada had it under control. He stopped them from doing anything more to Scarlett."

"Anything more?"

"They had cut her T-shirt off," Sam said.

"How bad did they hurt her?" Noah swallowed hard because he was scared to death to hear.

"They didn't get the chance. It was pure luck that I was at the office because of a report of an attempted robbery at the convenience store. I

168

called Brody in, then radioed Paul, and we were at the bar in no time."

"I need to go to her." Noah looked at the doctor.

"I can release you, but you have a lot of stitches, so you'll have to be extra careful."

"I will. I just need to get to her."

The doctor nodded. "I'll get your papers ready."

Noah leaned his head back and closed his eyes when he walked out of the room.

"Why don't you just marry that woman?"

Noah raised his head and looked at Sam.

"If she'll have me, I think I will."

"About damn time." Sam grinned.

"Where are they, Sam?" He squeezed Hailey's hand as she held onto it.

"In custody in Butte. Seems that little group has caused trouble across the state, and now it's caught up with them. They now have added charges against them. They won't be going anywhere for a long time."

"Good. I wanted to kill them."

"I'm sure you did. Little punk asses. You'll both have to testify against them, you know."

"With pleasure."

"All right, Mr. Conway, the nurse will be in with your instructions. I suggest you follow them because if you don't, you'll be right back in here," the doctor said as he reentered the room.

A while later, Noah stood at the doors to Dewey's but couldn't seem to open them. He glanced around to see the parking lot full. The place was always busy, even for a Wednesday night. He could hear laughter and conversations flowing. Would Scarlett be at the bar or upstairs?

"Only one way to find out," he muttered as he pulled the handle and opened the door.

Weaving through the crowd, he did his best not to let anyone run into him and made his way to the bar, then took a seat. He looked at the bartenders, but he didn't see her. He saw Keith coming toward him, stopping to give someone a beer on the way.

"Noah, it's great to see you. How are you doing?"

"I'm good, Keith. Uh, where's Scarlett?"

"Upstairs. She's taking a few nights off. Can I get you something?"

"Not yet." Noah put his hands on the bar and pushed to his feet. He winced at the pain but straightened up. "I'll just go up to see Scarlett."

"Uh, Noah? She said she didn't want to be disturbed."

"Too damn bad, Keith. Do you want to try and stop me? I might be in pain, but I could still probably kick your ass."

"I'm just telling you what she said. I like my job, Noah. Don't get me fired."

"I won't. She knows me well enough to know I won't stay away."

Noah slowly made his way through the crowd, again careful not to bump into anyone and back outside. It was too loud inside to try to knock on that door, so he'd go around to the back and go up that way. He gingerly made his way up the metal stairs. Each step brought another pain to his gut.

When he finally reached the top, he was sweating, even though it was below thirty. He had to stop and take deep breaths. The pain was excruciating. Part of the instructions had been not to climb a flight of stairs. *So what does he do? Climbs a fucking flight of stairs.*

After the pain subsided, he knocked on the door, and a few seconds later, the outside light came on, and he heard her unlocking the bolts. The door opened, and she stood with the light behind her.

"Noah, what are you doing out of the hospital?"

"Why didn't you visit me?"

"I did. You were always asleep. You had to know I'd be there."

"Can I come in? I need to sit down."

"Yes, of course." She opened the door wider, and he made his way past her.

He slowly walked to the sofa and gingerly lowered himself onto it. He leaned his head back and closed his eyes.

"Are you all right? Why are you out of the hospital?"

"Yes, I'm all right, and I was discharged."

"Shouldn't you be in bed?"

He opened one eye and grinned. "You gonna be there with me?"

"Noah Conway, you know that is not going to happen."

He opened his other eye and raised his head to look at her.

"Why not? Are you still going to marry Crawford?"

"No."

"Why not?"

"Because I don't love him."

"Good enough reason, I suppose."

"Noah, seriously, you should be resting. You shouldn't be here."

"I had to come here to apologize to you."

Scarlett took a seat beside him on the couch.

"Apologize for what?"

"If I hadn't pushed Powers, none of it would have happened."

"I don't blame you for any of it, Noah. You should know that."

He stared at her. She was so beautiful, and damn it, she was his. Not Crawford's or any other man who might want her. His. *Only* his. He reached his hand out to touch her soft hair. Taking a few strands in his fingers, he rubbed them together.

"Noah, please just lay down for a while. You just got out of the hospital. You need to rest."

"Give me a few minutes, and I'll go. I just wanted to say how sorry I am. They could have raped you, and it was all because of me."

Her hands cupped his cheeks. "No. I don't believe that. They were looking for trouble, and we just happened to be the ones they found it with. It wasn't anything you did. I would hope anyone would have stood up to them the way you did."

"Yeah, but I egged Powers on, and he wanted to get back at me by going after you. Sam told me they were wanted for all types of crimes across the state. When Powers stabbed me, and I fell, I wanted to get up so bad. I wanted to kill him, but I couldn't move, then I passed out."

"I know. I was so afraid you were going to die." A tear slid down her cheek.

Noah wiped it away with his thumb.

"The only way I'm going to die is if you tell me you don't want me anymore."

"I will always want you."

"There is no other woman for me, Scarlett. You're all I want. You have to know that."

"I know you want me…"

"I want you for the rest of my life. I'm not doing this very well." He tried to sit up but hissed in a breath at the pain.

"Noah, please, just lay back. I'll take care of you tonight."

"Not good enough, baby. I want you to take care of me for as long as I live. I love you, Scarlett. How could you not know that?"

"What?" Her mouth went slack.

"I love you." He stared into her eyes and watched as another tear rolled down her cheek. "You didn't know?"

"How could I? All you ever talked about was not settling down, so how would I know you loved me?"

"For God's sake, woman, I showed you in every way I could."

"Except by telling me."

"Touché." He grinned. "Well, I'm telling you now."

"I love you too, but then, you know that."

"I do." He cupped her face in his hands. "I want to marry you."

"You do?"

"Oh, yes, ma'am. I about died when you told me Crawford wanted to marry you, and when you said you were going to, I wanted to beat him to a pulp."

Scarlett laughed. "You've been getting violent lately, Noah Conway."

"Only if it involves my woman, and you *are* my woman, Scarlett. You have been since the first time you served me a beer. I love you, sweetheart, so very much."

Scarlett wound her arms around his neck and pressed her lips to his. He deepened it until she moaned into his mouth.

"Too bad we can't go to bed, and I'm not talking about sleeping." Noah grinned.

"We have our whole future ahead of us, but we are going to bed now to sleep. I'm tired, and you must be too. Did you bring your pain meds with you?"

"I did."

"Good." She stood and put her hand out to him. "Come on, let's go to bed."

Noah slowly got to his feet, took her hand, and let her lead him to her bedroom.

****

Later, Scarlett woke up and glanced around the room. The moonlight coming through the sheer curtains lit up the room.

"Are you all right?" Noah said from beside her.

"I've had some trouble sleeping since all of that happened," she whispered.

"He'll never lay a hand on you again, Scarlett. I promise you that." Noah kissed the top of her head.

"I'm pretty sure I would have killed him myself if you had died. I was so scared, Noah."

His arms tightened around her. "I wanted to kill him when he hit you. That little prick and his buddies are going away for a long time."

"He was so cocky."

"I'm sorry," Noah murmured.

"Noah, it is not your fault. I was just as bad. I let him know I wasn't interested in him at all, but men like him don't care what a woman says," she said.

"He's no man. He's a punk."

"I'm so glad that Nevada was smart enough to check on the bar lights being on."

"Hell, so am I. That's a cop's instinct."

"You should have seen him. I can't believe he walked right up to Powers and put that gun to his forehead," she said, shaking her head.

"He's a damn good deputy, but you shouldn't have come running out the door in the first place."

Scarlett sat up and stared down at him. "What was I supposed to do? Let them kill you?"

"I don't know, but maybe I could have gotten to one of them enough to make them back off."

"Noah, then they would have just kept trying to get to both of us."

"That's true. I didn't like Powers touching you."

"As you said, he never will again."

"What about Crawford?"

"I told him I couldn't marry him. I knew, even if you never married me, I'd only love you, and I'd take you any way I could get you."

Noah pushed her hair behind her ear. "How did he take it?"

"Surprisingly well. I think he's going to try to work it out with his ex-wife. I can tell he still loves her. Laura was right when she told me that Granger and I would end up divorced because I

175

loved you too much." She shook her head. "I don't know what I was thinking."

"You wanted to get married and have a family."

Scarlett lay back down and put her head on his chest.

"I do, but if you don't want to get married, Noah, that's fine. We can still be together. Laura reminded me about Kurt Russell and Goldie Hawn never marrying, and they've been together for years."

Noah chuckled. "Yeah, they have, but we're getting married, Scarlett. I want you to have my name, and I do want kids. I'd love to show them how to make saddles and pass that down to them."

"Sounds wonderful," she murmured and yawned.

"Let's get some sleep, baby."

"Do you need a pain pill?"

"As much as I hate taking them, yeah."

"I'll get it." She rolled away from him, got out of the bed, and strode to the bathroom to get a glass of water. She reentered the bedroom with the glass, handed it to him, opened the pill bottle, shook one out, and handed it to him. He tossed the pill into his mouth, took a sip of water, and handed the glass back to her. She set it on the nightstand then walked around the bed to crawl back in beside him.

"Thank you," he said.

"You needed to take it."

"No, I was thanking you for walking across the room naked." He chuckled when she laughed.

"I love you, Noah Conway," she whispered.

"I love you, Scarlett Robinson. We'll be fine."

"Yes, we will. You know, if you're so worried about being engaged, let's just go to the courthouse Monday and get married. There's no waiting period in Montana."

She sat up again and looked at him when he didn't answer.

"Are you serious?" he asked her.

"Yes."

"Wouldn't you rather get married in a church?"

"Why? People get married outside, so why does it matter?"

"I never thought of it like that, but we'll do whatever you want, baby. I know you'll go through with it."

"You're damn right I will, Noah. I have waited a long time to find the right man, and that's you."

"You just let me know what you decide, and we'll do it."

Scarlett nibbled on her lip. "To be honest, I would like to get married in a church because I'd want our families there."

Noah chuckled. "Then that's what we'll do. Now, come here, and let's get back to sleep."

She placed her head on his chest and ran her fingers through the hair there. She knew he trusted her enough not to leave him. After what they had been through, nothing was going to tear them apart. She glanced down to see the stitches to the right of his stomach. He had come so close to dying, and she knew then she would stay with him if he survived. However long he wanted her.

****

The light streaming through the window woke

him up. Noah blinked his eyes then remembered he was at Scarlett's apartment. He glanced to his side, but the bed was empty.

He started to get up and hissed in a breath at the pain in his side.

"Stay there," Scarlett said as she entered the room.

"I have to use the bathroom."

"Let me help you, Noah." Scarlett moved to the side of the bed, put her hands around his bicep, and gently pulled as he rolled to his side.

"Okay, give me a minute," he said, taking deep breaths.

"I'm sorry that hurts." She took a seat beside him, leaned over, and kissed his cheek.

"It's fine, darlin'. I'll mend." He kissed her forehead then leaned back to look at her when he felt her shaking. "Scarlett?"

"I was so scared, Noah. I was so afraid you were going to die."

He wrapped his arms around her as she sobbed.

"You're not getting rid of me that easily," he whispered.

Scarlett leaned back and looked up at him.

"I never want to get rid of you. I love you so much, Noah."

"I love you too." He gingerly got to his feet.

"Are you going to make it there?"

"You could help me to the door."

"Of course." She stood, wrapped her arms around his waist, and walked him to the door of the bathroom. "Do you need my help?"

Noah glanced down at her and could tell she was trying not to grin.

"If I let you help me, I'll be in worse shape than I am now because my dick will be hard, and I won't be able to do anything about it."

She burst out laughing. "Only you, Noah Conway. Only you."

"What?" he asked as he raised his eyebrows and chuckled when she laughed again. He kissed her forehead. "I'll be out in a minute."

"All right. I'll be in the living room." She turned to leave.

"Scarlett?"

"Yes?" She turned around to face him.

"Pack a bag, darlin', let's go home." He watched her blink tears from her eyes.

"I like the sound of that." She stood on her toes, kissed his chin, and walked back to the bedroom.

With a grin, Noah entered the bathroom. He was going to take everyone's advice and marry that woman. He wanted her with him all the time. It was time to take her home where she belonged.

****

A week later, Scarlett was behind the bar, serving drinks. Between her, Laura, and Keith, they were being run ragged.

"Is it me, or are we especially busy tonight?" Laura asked her as she poured a beer from the tap.

"It's not you. I suppose since we had a break in the weather, everyone got out of the house." Scarlett made a mixed drink.

"Can I take my break?"

Scarlett glanced over her shoulder to see Marie standing there.

"No. Not for a while. We're too busy right now," Scarlett told her.

"I get a fifteen-minute break," Marie snapped.

Scarlett set the drink on the bar in front of the customer then looked at Marie.

"You get a break when I say you do. Look around Marie. We are extremely busy. I can't spare you right now, not even for fifteen minutes."

"Fine." Marie spun around, picked up a tray with drinks on it, and made her way through the crowd.

"What was that about?" Laura asked her.

"Nothing. I need her too much right now," Scarlett told her. "Once it slows down, she can, but not now."

"Are you all right? You've been acting different around Marie lately."

"I'm fine." She looked at Laura. "Really. For some reason, my patience is running thin with her."

"Okay. I need to get this beer to the customer."

Scarlett nodded, but Laura had already turned away. She just wasn't sure what the hell was going on with Jeb, and he wasn't even here tonight. Maybe she should have let Marie take her break. Maybe Scarlett was wrong about those two. God, she hoped so.

She turned to look for Marie when she spotted Noah at the bar and made her way to him.

"Hi," she said.

"Hi, baby. Can I get a beer?"

Scarlett frowned. "Sure. Bottle or tap?"

"Either is fine." He spun around on the stool and watched the crowd.

He seemed distant for some reason, and if he was going to break it off with her, she would kick his ass. She got him a bottle of beer, twisted the cap off, and set it in front of him.

"Are you okay?"

Noah turned around and looked at her.

"Yeah, why?"

"I don't know..."

"I'm fine, Scarlett." He grinned.

"All right. Let me know if you need anything else."

"Yes, ma'am." He picked up the bottle then spun back around on the stool.

She wasn't sure what was going through his head, and it scared her. About an hour later, she glanced his way to see him jerk his chin for her, and she made her way to him.

"Need another?"

"No, I'm heading home. I'll see you when you get there." He pushed to his feet.

"Noah?"

"Yeah?"

"You're sure you're all right? Is your incision bothering you?"

"Not at all. I'm fine. I'll see you later." He leaned over the bar and gave her lips a quick kiss, and strode out of the bar.

She watched him go and jerked when someone touched her arm, and she looked over to see Laura.

"What's up?"

"Noah seems...distant. God, Laura, if he's running scared again, I will kick his ass. No questions asked."

"I hope not. You two have come through a lot.

181

Maybe—"

"Now, can I take a break?" Marie asked Scarlett.

"Yes, no more than fifteen, though."

"No problem."

Scarlett shook her head. "I have to stop imagining things."

"Yeah, you do. I'm sure Noah is just tired, but he did come in to see you," Laura said and turned away to wait on people.

Scarlett wasn't talking about Noah, but she sure couldn't tell Laura that. She was hoping she was wrong about Jeb and Marie. He hadn't been in all night. Shaking her head, she knew Jeb loved Laura.

Huffing out a breath, she got back to work. This night needed to end so she could find out what was going through Noah's mind because something sure was.

When she got home around three-thirty, the lights inside were on, and she knew he had waited up for her like he usually did. She parked her SUV, climbed out, walked up the steps, wiped her feet, and entered the house. She smiled when Sparky and Spike ran to her. Squatting down, she hugged them and kissed their snouts.

"Hey."

She looked up to see Noah standing in the kitchen doorway, leaning against the jamb. He never moved. She straightened up, removed her coat, hung it on the pegs then walked to him.

"What's going on through that head of yours, Noah?"

His eyebrows shot up. "What do you mean?"

"You just seemed distant at the bar earlier. Are you rethinking this?" She waved her hand between them.

She quickly blinked as tears formed when he didn't say anything. Then he pulled her into his arms, and she wrapped hers around his waist. She felt him kiss the top of her head.

"I told you that I wanted to spend my life with you, Scarlett."

"But—"

"I went into the bar because I wanted to be with you, and—"

Scarlett pulled back from him and looked up into his handsome face.

"And, what?"

"Nothing. Just be with you."

She didn't think he was telling her everything, but unless he told her what was going through his head, she had to believe he was just there to be with her.

"All right, Noah." She took his hand. "Let's go to bed. I'm so tired."

"I am too. It's been a long damn day."

"I concluded that I was wrong about Jeb. He wasn't even there tonight, and Marie was. I just let my imagination run away."

"I'm glad to hear that."

They entered the bedroom then Scarlett headed for the bathroom to shower. Something still didn't seem right with Noah, though. She was sure her imagination wasn't wrong on *that*.

As she stood in the shower, she saw him enter the bathroom, strip off his sweatpants and T-shirt. He opened the door and stepped in behind her. She turned to wrap her arms around his waist and raised her face for him to kiss her. He kissed her long and deep, then raised his lips from hers and stared into her eyes.

"I need you," he said.

"I need you too." She gasped when he lifted her, put her back against the wall, and slid into her when she wrapped her legs around his waist. "Don't hurt yourself."

"I'm fine," he whispered in her ear.

Scarlett held on as he thrust hard into her, withdrew, and thrust in again. Over and over. He pressed his lips to hers again just as her orgasm rushed over her, and she screamed into his mouth. He groaned and followed her over. When he raised his head, she looked into his eyes.

"I love you, Scarlett," he said.

"I love you too," she whispered.

Later as they lay in bed, she knew he was asleep by his deep, even breathing.

"He said he loved you. Stop imagining the worst," she whispered.

His arms tightened around her. She should just stop thinking altogether.

"We're fine, darlin'," he said.

She snuggled against him and smiled. He did love her. She knew that with all her heart.

****

Noah watched Scarlett set another drink on the bar in front of a young woman, take her money, then turn to the cash register. She saw him and walked to where he sat.

"Hey, cowboy," she said.

"Hey, darlin'."

"I didn't think you were coming in tonight."

"I wasn't, but I missed you. Is that all right?"

184

"Of course. You can come in here anytime." She leaned over the bar. "If you drink too much, we'll just stay upstairs. You know I love climbing those stairs with you." She ran her fingers through the hair on his forearm.

"Shit, you're going to make my dick hard, Scarlett, but I did like going up those stairs too. Fuck, that was hot."

"No reason we can't do it again. I know you don't have stairs at your house, but we can always use those," she said as she jerked her thumb over her shoulder toward the hallway that led to the door of her apartment.

"I'm all for that."

"Do you want a beer?"

"Sure. Bottle is fine." He stared into her eyes.

"I'll be right back." She walked to the cooler, removed a beer, twisted the cap off, walked back to him, and set it down in front of him. "Anything else?"

Noah took her hand in his. "Yes."

"What?"

"You know when you kept asking me if I was all right the other night?" When she nodded, he went on. "Well, I wasn't."

"What is it?"

"I had to get my courage up." He shook his head.

"Courage for what?" she asked him, and he knew she was thinking he was going to break it off with her.

"Give me your other hand," he said.

Scarlett frowned at him but placed her hand in his. He reached into his coat and pulled out a little black velvet box. She put her hand over her mouth.

"Noah, what are you doing?"

"I'm officially asking you to marry me. I know you won't take this ring off until I slide a wedding band on this finger. I trust you with all my heart, and I want to share my life with you and the children we have."

"I don't know what to say," she said.

"Say yes." Noah opened the lid to show her a three-carat princess cut diamond set in yellow gold. "If you don't like it, we can return it and get one you do like."

"I love it," she said as tears rolled down her cheeks.

Noah removed the ring, lifted her left hand, slid the ring on her finger, and kissed her knuckles. She leaned over the bar, cupped his face in her hands, and kissed him. The crowd along the bar cheered.

"I didn't hear a yes," he said.

"Yes! Of course, yes," she cried.

"Hell, don't scare me like that. That's why I was trying to gain courage. I was so afraid you'd say no."

"You should know I wouldn't say no. I thought you were going to break it off with me."

"No way. I love you too much not to have you in my life." He watched her blink tears from her eyes. He knew she loved him and always would.

"I love you, Noah."

"I love you too, darlin'." He got to his feet, leaned over the bar, and took her lips in a deep kiss making everyone cheer. He raised his lips slowly and stared into her eyes. "I think we need to use those steps again tonight." He grinned when she laughed.

"Anytime, baby, anytime," she whispered and pressed her lips to his again.

Noah chuckled when she raised her lips from his.

"I'll be there." He winked.

She smiled then leaned back from him. "I have to get to work. You just sit right here and wait."

"I'll try." He grinned. "Hey, what time do you get a break?"

Scarlett burst out laughing. Life would never be dull with her. She meant everything to him, and he couldn't wait to spend the rest of his life with her. Saying she was the best thing that ever happened to him would be a huge understatement. She winked at him.

"I'll let you know." She moved along the bar, refilling drinks.

He hoped that break came sooner than later, he thought with a grin.

Epilogue

"Did you invite everyone from all three towns?" Noah asked.

Scarlett shrugged. "I didn't want to leave anyone out."

He chuckled. "I think you achieved that."

Taking her hand in his, they made their way through the crowd to the bar. They were stopped along the way so people could shake their hands, hug, and congratulate them. Noah grinned when he saw Trick heading for him and stuck his hand out. Trick shook it.

"It wasn't so hard, was it?" Trick asked him.

"No. I was running scared," Noah said with a grin.

"Hell, I know what that's like, but we all have to take a chance, Noah." Trick glanced at Rayna and Scarlett, talking then back to him. "I can't imagine not having her in my life. Everyone knows how much I loved Kaylee, and her death devastated me, but I also knew she would never want me to do anything drastic and to move on."

"I get that too. Scarlett means everything to me. I was just stubborn."

Scarlett turned to look up at him. "You? Stubborn? What an understatement, Conway."

Noah and Trick laughed, then Trick gave him a nod, took Rayna's hand, and made their way to a table. Noah pulled Scarlett against him, lowered his head, and kissed her long and slow. She pulled back, laughed against his lips, then he raised his head and stared into her eyes. The crowd whooped and hollered.

"You know, I'm still going to be stubborn."

"I wouldn't have you any other way," Scarlett said, staring up at him as she placed her hand on his cheek.

He kissed her forehead, took her hand, and led her to the bar, where they took seats on the stools. Laura made her way to them.

"What would you two like?"

"Laura, thank you so much for coming in to do this," Scarlett said.

"Of course. Dewey, Keith, and I are doing fine. I'm just glad that Allie and Carrie were willing to come in on a Sunday."

"I am too." Scarlett glanced around. "I can't believe the crowd."

"It's your engagement party, so of course, everyone came." Laura winked.

Noah and Scarlett gave her their order, and she walked off to get it. Noah turned on the stool, looked at the crowd, and shook his head.

"Tell everyone it's an open bar, and they crawl out of the woodwork," he said.

"You didn't have to do that, Noah," Scarlett touched his hand.

"I wanted to. We wanted to celebrate with everyone. It's not like I can't afford it, darlin'." He kissed her temple.

"I know, but—"

"No buts, Scarlett. It's fine. I've known most of these people my entire life. I'm glad they showed up." He grinned when he saw Boone Evans making his way through the crowd to him, pulling his fiancée, Sandy Barnes, behind him.

"Noah," Boone said as he put his hand out for Noah to shake.

Noah got to his feet, shook Boone's hand, and hugged Sandy.

"Glad you two could make it," Noah said.

"We wouldn't miss it," Sandy said and turned to hug Scarlett. "I'm so happy for you both."

"Thanks, Sandy. We're pretty happy too," Scarlett said with a grin.

"About time he came to his senses," Boone teased.

Noah snorted. "Yeah, like you jumped right in."

Boone and Sandy laughed. Boone glanced over his shoulder and back to Noah.

"It's good for everyone to get together once in a while."

"I agree." Noah jerked his chin at the stage. "I'm glad the band could play today."

"Hell, you know Devin and Jaxon asked them to do it." Boone looked at the stage.

The couples talked for a while before Sandy and Boone made their way back to a table. Noah looked down at Scarlett when she slid her arm through his.

"Thank you," she said.

"For what?"

"Everything." She shrugged. "This is amazing. I love your friends. They're all great."

"Yeah, they are," Noah said and chuckled when the crowd roared as Grant hopped up on the stage.

"Oh! Is he going to sing?" Scarlett murmured.

"Looks like it." Noah grinned.

Grant walked to the mic, grinned, and raised

his beer mug.

"To the happy couple, Noah and Scarlett. Took you long enough, buddy," he said, making the crowd laugh, then he picked up a guitar and sang with the band.

"Not everyone can say they had a country singer superstar sing at their engagement party." Noah shook his head.

"I will never forget this day," Scarlett said as she wrapped her arms around his waist.

"I won't either." Noah kissed the top of her head. "I should never have doubted you."

"Well, as you said, you are one stubborn man, Noah Conway, but I do love you."

"Damn good thing, baby." Noah looked down into her eyes.

He had no doubt this woman would always be at his side. He might be stubborn, but there were days where he had nothing on her. She didn't back down, and he loved that about her. He pulled her close, rested his chin on the top of her head, and watched people having a good time.

Mentally shaking his head, he wondered why he was ever scared of falling again. This would be the last time. He would love Scarlett for the rest of his life, and he knew she'd do the same with him. Yeah, he knew there was nothing to be afraid of. He grinned, just thinking about the future with her and the family they would create together. He couldn't wait for that.

Noah also knew that he and Scarlett would clash on things because both were beyond stubborn and hardheaded, but he loved the thought of making up. Maybe he needed to install some stairs in his house somewhere, he thought with a grin.

* * *The End* * *

About the Author

Susan was born and raised in Cumberland, MD. She moved to Tennessee in 1996 with her husband, and they now live in a small town outside of Nashville, along with their three dogs. She is a huge Nashville Predators hockey fan. She also enjoys fishing, taking drives down back roads, and visiting Gatlinburg, TN, her family in Pittsburgh, PA, and her hometown. Although Susan's books are a series, each book can be read as a standalone book. Each book will end with a HEA and a new story beginning in the next one. She would love to hear from her readers and promises to try to respond to all.

You can visit her website, Facebook page, Instagram, and email by the links below.
www.susanfisherdavisauthor.weebly.com
Susan Fisher-Davis, Romance
Author | Facebook
Susanfisherdavis_author
Email: susan@susanfisherdavisauthor.com

Made in the USA
Coppell, TX
28 February 2022

74224770R00115